E.G. Swain
BONE TO HIS BONE

MICHAEL COX has published several books relating to English supernatural fiction. He is the author of a widely-praised biography of M.R. James (*M.R. James: An Informal Portrait*, Oxford, 1983; Oxford Paperbacks, 1986) and has edited two selections of James's ghost stories: *The Ghost Stories of M.R. James* (Oxford, 1986) and *M.R. James: 'Casting the Runes' and Other Ghost Stories* (Oxford: The World's Classics, 1987). He is also co-editor of *The Oxford Book of English Ghost Stories* (1986) and has produced an illustrated selection of the ghost stories and mysteries of J.S. Le Fanu (Equation, 1988).

Also available in this series

The Flint Knife: Further Spook Stories by E.F. Benson
Selected and introduced by Jack Adrian

In the Dark: Tales of Terror by E. Nesbit
Selected and introduced by Hugh Lamb

Warning Whispers: Weird Tales by A.M. Burrage
Selected and introduced by Jack Adrian

The Magic Mirror: Lost Supernatural Tales by Algernon Blackwood
Selected and introduced by Michael Ashley

Stories in the Dark: Tales of Terror by Jerome K. Jerome, Robert Barr, and Barry Pain
Selected and introduced by Hugh Lamb

The Black Reaper: Tales of Terror by Bernard Capes
Introduced by Hugh Lamb

Dracula's Brood: Rare Vampire Stories
Selected and introduced by Richard Dalby

BONE TO HIS BONE

The Stoneground Ghost Tales of E.G. Swain

Introduced by

MICHAEL COX

First published as *The Stoneground Ghost Tales*, 1912
This edition first published 1989

British Library Cataloguing in Publication Data

Swain, E.G. (Edmund Gill)
Bone to his bone
I. Title
823'.912 [F]

ISBN 1-85336-097-X

Equation is part of the Thorsons Publishing Group Limited, Wellingborough, Northamptonshire, NN8 2RQ, England

Printed in Great Britain by Richard Clay Limited, Bungay, Suffolk

1 3 5 7 9 10 8 6 4 2

CONTENTS

TO

MONTAGUE RHODES JAMES

(LITT.D., HON. LITT.D. DUBLIN,
HON. LL.D. ST. ANDR., F.B.A, F.S.A, ETC.)
PROVOST OF KING'S COLLEGE, CAMBRIDGE,
FOR TWENTY PLEASANT YEARS MR BATCHEL'S FRIEND,
AND THE INDULGENT PARENT OF SUCH TASTES
AS THESE PAGES INDICATE

E.G. Swain

INTRODUCTION

THERE have been many ghost stories written in emulation of M.R. James, who is still, by almost unanimous critical consent, regarded as one of the most consistently accomplished writers of supernatural fiction of the twentieth century. But amongst the volumes written by James's many followers *The Stoneground Ghost Tales* of E.G. Swain hold a special place.

It was not just that James, who knew and liked Swain, was the acknowledged inspirer of the latter's stories, which were prominently and affectionately dedicated to James, 'the indulgent parent of such tastes as these pages indicate'. Swain's nine tales, first published by Heffers in 1912 and now amongst the rarest ghost-story collections in English, are far closer to James in spirit and ambience than any of his other admirers. Though they lack the unsettling, anarchic malevolence of James, whose ghosts often have a peculiarly loathsome palpability, Swain's tales share the same narrational qualities. The voice of the storyteller in *The Stoneground Ghost Tales* is recognizably from the same stock as that of James's stories, first heard by the general reading public in *Ghost Stories of an Antiquary* (1904). But then Swain enjoyed close contact with James over a decade and more: like another self-confessed Jamesian, R.H. Malden, Swain was able almost literally to sit at the feet of the Master.

Edmund Gill Swain was born in 1861, just a year before M.R.

James, the son of Charles Swain of Stockport in Cheshire. He was educated at Manchester Grammar School and in 1880 went up as Scholar to Emmanuel College, Cambridge, to read Natural Sciences. After taking a rather poor degree—a Third—he was ordained deacon in 1885 and priest the following year, at Rochester. He then took up a curacy at Camberwell until 1892, in which year he was appointed a Chaplain of King's College, Cambridge. For the next thirteen years Swain lived in college rooms at King's and held a number of posts in the university and the town, including Junior Proctor, Assistant Registrary, and, for nearly ten years, Hon. Secretary of the Charity Organization Society. 'When the present century began,' said the King's College Annual Report for 1938, 'there were in Cambridge few more familiar figures and not many men more respected and liked. The late Provost of Eton [i.e. M.R. James] was only an outstanding one among his near friends.'

When Swain first came to know M.R. James—'Monty' to his large circle of friends and admirers—James was Dean of King's and already one of the outstanding scholars of his generation. In October 1893, the year after Swain was admitted at King's, James read the first of his ghost stories, 'Lost Hearts' and 'Canon Alberic's Scrap-book', to the 601st meeting of the Chitchat Society. (Swain was not present on that historic occasion, though E.F. Benson, who was also to become a highly proficient—and prolific—writer of ghost stories, was.) The response of his immediate circle to the two stories was enthusiastic, and in time James obliged by writing further tales in the same antiquarian vein.

By the turn of the century a new ghost story by Monty James was eagerly expected by the select circle of friends invited to celebrate Christmas in the perfect surroundings of King's. In 1917 James's old Eton tutor, H.E. Luxmoore, recalled the highlights of these gatherings—'the walk in the Backs and the talk with ghosts and the sense of friendship and old days and above all the mystery of the beauty of Chapel . . .' James himself wistfully looked back to these Christmases, in the palmy days before the First World War, in his published recollections, *Eton and King's* (1926):

It would be Christmas Eve: we of the College surpliced ourselves and repaired to Chapel. Choir and ante-chapel were full, and dark. Just before the clock struck five the boys would issue from their vestry on the north side, the men from the Hacombleyn chantry on the south; last, the officers came from the Brassie chantry, and, led by Walter Littlechild with his silver verge, proceeded westwards and took their stand near the south door. A faint musical hum was heard, of the choir taking up the note, and then—it seemed to give the very spirit of Christmas—the boys broke quite softly into 'Once in Royal David's City', and began moving eastward. With the second verse the men joined in. I declare I do not know what has moved me more than this did, and still does when I recall it.

Dinner in Hall followed, at which hot spiced beer was served. Then there might be cards and, at last, the adjournment to Monty's rooms to hear the year's ghost story, often composed, according to James, 'at fever heat'. A typical reading was described in the unpublished recollections of Oliffe Richmond, who came up to King's from Eton in 1900:

Monty disappeared into his bedroom. We sat and waited in the candle-light. Perhaps someone played a few bars on the piano, and desisted, for good reason . . . The people in the room varied from year to year, but some of the following were sure to be present: Luxmoore . . . Gurney Lubbock . . . and (A.B) Ramsay, from Eton. Walter Morley Fletcher from Trinity; Owen Hugh Smith from London (he almost always); the Revd Swain, or his successor, F.E. Hutchinson, our Chaplain; (James) McBryde, the artist of the 'Troll Hunt' . . . perhaps Percy Lubbock or Arthur Benson had slipped in from Magdalene . . . Monty emerged from the bedroom, manuscript in hand, at last, and blew out all the candles but one, by which he seated himself. He then began to read, with more confidence than anyone else could have mustered, his well-nigh illegible script in the dim light.

Such was the success of James's stories that other members of the party tried their hand at writing and reading tales of a grim kind. In 1903, for instance, Arthur Benson followed Monty with one called 'The House at Trehele', published in 1927 as 'Basil Netherby'. And in due course Swain, though there is no record of his having contributed to the Christmas entertainments at King's, began to devise his own tales very much in the Jamesian manner.

Between Swain and James there was an easy, undemanding relationship—precisely the kind that suited James best. On Swain's side, there appears to have been a degree of hero worship (not uncommon amongst James's friends and acquaintances): certainly he had immense respect for James's scholarship, as well as for the fact that James represented the very best in traditional collegiate values. Swain spoke for many in Cambridge when he wrote to James in 1918 on the latter's appointment to the provostship of Eton:

> Cambridge will long be unsettled, and when settlement begins, a great deal of it will lie outside your main interests and sympathies . . . What many hundreds of us will feel is that it is the end, but for a few survivals, of King's as we knew it, you being a real link with the past. Your intellectual and other antecedents belonged to the King's of history, to enter into which has been the main pleasure and privilege of my life.

Though he was not an Etonian, which many of James's closest friends were, Swain nevertheless had the qualities of mind and disposition with which James felt comfortable. As well as a common conservative temperament, both men also shared a similar sense of humour. In the mid-1890s they had collaborated on what James called 'topical' (i.e. mildly satirical) plays, written for the amusement of the choristers over Christmas and performed at the ADC Theatre: *The Dismal Tragedy of Henry Blew Beard, Esq* (in which James took the title role) and a version of Ali Baba with the ludicrously plangent Latin title of *Historia de Alexandro Barberio et XL Latrionibus*. For these entertainments James wrote the scripts and Swain provided lyrics that were set to music by the organist of King's, Dr A.H. Mann.

Swain's antiquarian interests, though pursued strictly on an amateur level compared to James, also provided a point of contact. In *The Story of Peterborough Cathedral* (1932) Swain showed himself to be an able chronicler of the cathedral's history (and at one point—in connection with the Peterborough Psalter—he praises James's scholarship). Swain also appears to have been a keen Dickensian (the references in 'Lubrietta' to Mrs Gamp and Mr Pickwick are clear indications of this), as was James; and, like James, he never married.

In 1896, in addition to his duties as Chaplain of King's, Swain became curate of Great St Mary's, the University church. He remained in Cambridge until 1905 (the year M.R. James was elected Provost of King's), when he accepted the Emmanuel living of Stanground (then in Huntingdonshire). 'He worked there, among rough parishioners [said a King's obituary notice], with the simple and unostentatious devotion that marked his whole life, for eleven years.' In 1916—in need, it seems, of rest—he accepted the King's living of Greenford, then a quiet and comfortable rural parish, with its beautiful church. He left Greenford in 1923 and returned to Peterborough, this time to the cathedral where he filled a succession of posts: Minor Canon and Librarian 1923-31, Sacristan 1923-30, Honorary Canon 1926, and Precentor 1930-1. He continued to keep in touch with Monty James, visiting him at Eton, for instance, in June 1923. He died in the cathedral precincts on 29 January 1938, leaving the instruction that his former colleagues at King's should send no flowers for his grave.

It was Stanground—thinly disguised as Stoneground in the stories—that provided Swain with all the material he needed for his ghost stories. It stood 'on the edge of that vast tract of East Anglia, which retains its ancient name of the Fens'. Once a picturesque village, the 'unlovely signs of industry', the clay pits and sprouting chimneys, had changed the place 'alike in aspect and in population'. Close by the church of St John the Baptist (which is described in 'The Eastern Window') stood the vicarage with its spacious garden that features in several of the tales. In such a place the past would sometimes physically intrude into the present, as it did in 1907, during Swain's time as vicar, when a fragment of a thirteenth-century chalice was found in a stone coffin under the south aisle of the church—an incident that is perhaps relevant to the eighth story in this collection, 'The Place of Safety'.

The incumbent of the fictional parish, and the hero of the nine stories, is the Reverend Roland Batchel, described in the first adventure, 'The Man With the Roller', as 'a solitary man of somewhat studious habits', not unlike Swain himself. It is the genial figure of Mr Batchel that provides both continuity and human substance to *The Stoneground Ghost Tales*. In Mr Batchel, Swain managed to breathe real life into a character—the bachelor antiquarian—that in the stories of M.R. James is often a distant and detached figure. Not so Mr Batchel. With great economy of description, Swain invests his hero with real warmth and humanity. We quickly make the vicar's acquaintance and, just as quickly, are drawn into the world of Stoneground and its inhabitants—both living and dead. The critic Jack Sullivan, in his book *Elegant Nightmares*, rightly remarked that Mr Batchel is 'a winning creation':

> Intractably conservative, he is the perfect antiquary, a man who collects and arranges relics and artefacts, partly out of a worship of the past, partly out of a need to create the illusion that nothing is ever out of its place . . . [M.R.] James's collectors are much the same way, but we never get to know any one of them as well as we do Batchel.

For Batchel appears in all of the Stoneground tales, and he encounters in that haunted parish some of the most memorable ghosts in fiction.

Swain is adept, too, at bringing his subsidiary characters to life with a few deft touches. Take Mrs Rumney, 'who had once been young' (what a wonderfully compressed and appropriate phrase that is) and who is content to wait upon her lodger, the photographer Mr Groves, 'chemical though he may be', because he is 'a nice gentleman, AND a gentleman'. Or Mr Mutcher, the Deputy Provincial Grand Master of the Antient Order of Gleaners (the DPGM for short), in 'The Indian Lampshade', who descends unwelcomingly on Mr Batchel one frosty Janaury evening to discuss the probable effect of the Insurance Act on Friendly Societies. Mr Mutcher is obliged to cut short his visit when he sees an elderly gentleman (certainly not of this world) enter the room carrying a box which he proceeds to place on what the vicar's guest calls 'the sheffoneer'. At the end of the story Mr Batchel calls on the DPGM, who expresses the hope that he will be allowed to resume his discourse on the subject of National Insurance:

'I shall not have much leisure,' said Mr Batchel, audaciously, taking all risks, 'until the Greek Kalends.'*

'Oh, I don't mind waiting till it does end,' said Mr Mutcher, 'there is no immediate 'urry.'

'It's rather a long time,' remarked Mr Batchel.

'Pray don't mention it,' answered the Deputy Provincial Grand Master, in his best manner. 'But when the time comes, perhaps you'll drop me a line.'

Even the spooks can engage our sympathies. The title story of this edition, 'Bone to His Bone', perhaps shows Swain at his best in this respect. Here historical fact and private fiction are nicely

*i.e. never. The Greeks did not have Kalends.

intermingled in the figure of William Whitehead, an actual Vicar of Stanground who died in 1754 and who was a Fellow of Swain's own college, Emmanuel. In this tale the dead and the living confront each other in a genuinely touching way. Nevertheless, Swain is still able to conjure up a scene that is likely to produce an unexpected *frisson* in the reader:

> The moon, by this time, had passed out of the south, and the library seemed all the darker by contrast with the moonlit chamber he had left. He could see nothing but two blue-grey rectangles formed by the windows against the sky, the furniture of the room being altogether invisible. Groping along to where the table stood, Mr Batchel felt over its surface for the matches which usually lay there; he found, however, that the table was cleared of everything. He raised his right hand, therefore, in order to feel his way to a shelf where the matches were sometimes mislaid, and at that moment, whilst his hand was in mid-air, the matchbox was gently put into it!

This is a good example of what Jack Sullivan called the 'delicate texture of spookiness which gives Swain a voice of his own'. It is a voice which a small band of Swain enthusiasts have learned to savour and admire, and regret that its owner was not more prolific. Though it is unlikely that any new stories by E.G. Swain will ever come to light, Mr Batchel's friends can at least take pleasure in the six stories by David Rowlands printed at the end of this volume. They are the nearest thing to the spirit and humour of the originals that one could possibly hope for and they deserve a wide audience, both as excellent tales in their own right and as tributes to Mr Batchel's creator. I am grateful to David Rowlands for so kindly allowing them to be reprinted here.

If nothing else, *The Stoneground Ghost Tales* demonstrate the variety of supernatural fiction in English, for here are stories that stand in direct contrast to the blatant horrors of such practitioners as E.F. Benson, H. Russell Wakefield, or even, on occasion, M.R. James; and yet, like all the great exponents of the genre, Swain creates credible interactions between the past and the present, between the living and the dead. That he does so with restraint and humour only adds to his achievement.

The chills, then, are here, from the appearance of the 'creamy vaporous figure' in 'The Eastern Window' to the violent ghost of an eighteenth-century suicide in 'The Rockery'. But there is much more besides, making *The Stoneground Ghost Tales* one of the most delightful and satisfying rarities in English supernatural fiction. As to the question, did E.G. Swain believe in ghosts, there is sadly no definitive answer. It seems likely that he shared Mr Batchel's attitude of 'humble curiosity'; perhaps, like the vicar of Stoneground, 'he refused even to guess why the *revenant* was sometimes invisible, and at other times partly or wholly visible; sometimes capable of using physical force, and at other times powerless. He knew that they had their periods, and that was all.'

Whatever their author's views on the subject, *The Stoneground Ghost Tales* have been neglected for far too long. I hope that with this new edition these romances of the invisible world will find the audience they deserve.

Michael Cox

THE MAN WITH THE ROLLER

ON the edge of that vast tract of East Anglia, which retains its ancient name of the Fens, there may be found, by those who know where to seek it, a certain village called Stoneground. It was once a picturesque village. Today it is not to be called either a village, or picturesque. Man dwells not in one 'house of clay', but in two, and the material of the second is drawn from the earth upon which this and the neighbouring villages stood. The unlovely signs of the industry have changed the place alike in aspect and in population. Many who have seen the fossil skeletons of great saurians brought out of the clay in which they have lain from prehistoric times, have thought that the inhabitants of the place have not since changed for the better. The chief habitations, however, have their foundations not upon clay, but upon a bed of gravel which anciently gave to the place its name, and upon the highest part of this gravel stands, and has stood for many centuries, the parish church, dominating the landscape for miles around.

Stoneground, however, is no longer the inaccessible village, which in the middle ages stood out above a waste of waters. Occasional floods serve to indicate what was once its ordinary outlook, but in more recent times the construction of roads and railways, and the drainage of the Fens, have given it freedom of communication with the world from which it was formerly isolated.

The Vicarage of Stoneground stands hard by the church, and is renowned for its spacious garden, part of which, and that (as might be expected) the part nearest the house, is of ancient date. To the original plot successive vicars have added adjacent lands, so that the garden has gradually acquired the state in which it now appears.

The vicars have been many in number. Since Henry de Greville was instituted in the year 1140 there have been 30, all of whom have lived, and most of whom have died, in successive vicarage houses upon the present site.

The present incumbent, Mr Batchel, is a solitary man of somewhat studious habits, but is not too much enamoured of his solitude to receive visits, from time to time, from schoolboys and such. In the summer of the year 1906 he entertained two, who are the occasion of this narrative, though still unconscious of their part in it, for one of the two, celebrating his fifteenth birthday during his visit to Stoneground, was presented by Mr Batchel with a new camera, with which he proceeded to photograph, with considerable skill, the surroundings of the house.

One of these photographs Mr Batchel thought particularly pleasing. It was a view of the house with the lawn in the foreground. A few small copies, such as the boy's camera was capable of producing, were sent to him by his young friend, some weeks after the visit, and again Mr Batchel was so much pleased with the picture, that he begged for the negative, with the intention of having the view enlarged.

The boy met the request with what seemed a needlessly modest plea. There were two negatives, he replied, but each of them had, in the same part of the picture, a small blur for which there was no accounting otherwise than by carelessness. His desire, therefore, was to discard these films, and to produce something more worthy of enlargement, upon a subsequent visit.

Mr Batchel, however, persisted in his request, and upon receipt of the negative, examined it with a lens. He was just able to detect the blur alluded to; an examination under a powerful glass, in fact revealed something more than he had at first detected. The blur was like the nucleus of a comet as one sees it represented in pictures, and seemed to be connected with a faint streak which extended across the negative. It was, however, so inconsiderable a defect that Mr Batchel resolved to disregard it. He had a neighbour whose favourite pastime was photography, one who was notable skilled in everything that pertained to the art, and to him he sent the negative, with the request for an enlargement, reminding him of a long-standing promise to do any such service, when as had now happened, his friend might see fit to ask it.

This neighbour who had acquired such skill in photography was one Mr Groves, a young clergyman, residing in the precincts of the Minster near at hand, which was visible from Mr Batchel's garden. He lodged with a Mrs Rumney, a superannuated servant of the Palace, and a strong-minded vigorous woman still, exactly such a one as Mr Groves needed to have about him. For he was a constant trial to Mrs Rumney, and but for the wholesome fear she begot in him, would have converted his rooms into a mere den. Her carpets and tablecloths were continually bespattered with chemicals; her chimney-piece ornaments had been unceremoniously stowed away and replaced by labelled bottles; even the bed of Mr Groves was, by day, strewn with drying films and mounts, and her old and favourite cat had a bald patch on his flank, the result of a mishap with the pyrogallic acid.

Mrs Rumney's lodger, however, was a great favourite with her, as such helpless men are apt to be with motherly women, and she took no small pride in his work. A life-size portrait of herself, originally a peace-offering, hung in her parlour, and had long excited the envy of every friend who took tea with her.

'Mr Groves,' she was wont to say, 'is a nice gentleman, AND a gentleman; and chemical though he may be, I'd rather wait on him for nothing than what I would on anyone else for twice the money.'

Every new piece of photographic work was of interest to Mrs Rumney, and she expected to be allowed both to admire and to criticize. The view of Stoneground Vicarage, therefore, was shown to her upon its arrival. 'Well may it want enlarging,' she remarked, 'and it no bigger than a postage stamp; it looks more like a doll's house than a vicarage,' and with this she went about her work, whilst Mr Groves retired to his darkroom with the film, to see what he could make of the task assigned to him.

Two days later, after repeated visits to his darkroom, he had made something considerable; and when Mrs Rumney brought him his chop for luncheon, she was lost in admiration. A large but unfinished print stood upon his easel, and such a picture of Stoneground Vicarage was in the making as was calculated to delight both the young photographer and the vicar.

Mr Groves spent only his mornings, as a rule, in photography. His afternoons he gave to pastoral work, and the work upon this enlargement was over for the day. It required little more than 'touching up', but it was this 'touching up' which made the difference between the enlargements of Mr Groves and those of the other men. The print, therefore, was to be left upon the easel until the morrow, when it was to be finished. Mrs Rumney and he, together, gave it an admiring inspection as she was carrying away the tray, and what they agreed in admiring most particularly was the smooth and open stretch of lawn, which made so excellent a foreground for the picture. 'It looks,' said Mrs Rumney, who had once been young, 'as if it was waiting for someone to come and dance on it.'

Mr Groves left his lodgings—we must now be particular about the hours—at half-past two, with the intention of returning, as usual, at five. 'As reg'lar as a clock,' Mrs Rumney was wont to say, 'and a sight more reg'lar than some clocks I know of.'

Upon this day he was, nevertheless, somewhat late, some visit had detained him, unexpectedly, and it was a quarter-past five when he inserted his latchkey in Mrs Rumney's door.

Hardly had he entered, when his landlady, obviously awaiting him, appeared in the passage: her face, usually florid, was of the colour of parchment, and, breathing hurriedly and shortly, she pointed at the door of Mr Groves' room.

In some alarm at her condition, Mr Groves hastily questioned her; all she could say was: 'The photograph! The photograph!' Mr Groves could only suppose that his enlargement had met with some mishap for which Mrs Rumney was responsible. Perhaps she had allowed it to flutter into the fire. He turned towards his room in order to discover the worst, but at this Mrs Rumney laid a trembling hand upon his arm, and held him back. 'Don't go in,' she said, 'have your tea in the parlour.'

'Nonsense,' said Mr Groves, 'if that is gone we can easily do another.'

'Gone,' said his landlady, 'I wish to heaven it was.'

The ensuing conversation shall not detain us. It will suffice to say that after a considerable time Mr Groves succeeded in quieting his landlady, so much so that she consented, still trembling violently, to enter the room with him. To speak truth, she was as much concerned for him as for herself, and she was not by nature a timid woman.

The room, so far from disclosing to Mr Groves any cause for excitement, appeared wholly unchanged. In its usual place stood every article of his stained and ill-used furniture, on the easel stood the photograph, precisely where he had left it; and except that his tea was not upon the table, everything was in its usual state and place.

But Mrs Rumney again became excited and tremulous. 'It's there,' she cried. 'Look at the lawn.'

Mr Groves stepped quickly forward and looked at the photograph. Then he turned as pale as Mrs Rumney herself.

There was a man, a man with an indescribably horrible suffering face, rolling the lawn with a large roller.

Mr Groves retreated in amazement to where Mrs Rumney had remained standing. 'Has anyone been in here?' he asked.

'Not a soul,' was the reply, 'I came in to make up the fire, and turned to have another look at the picture, when I saw that dead-alive face at the edge. It gave me the creeps,' she said, 'particularly from not having noticed it before. If that's anyone in Stoneground, I said to myself, I wonder the vicar has him in the garden with that awful face. It took that hold of me I thought I must come and look at it again, and at five o'clock I brought your tea in. And then I saw him moved along right in front, with a roller dragging behind him, like you see.'

Mr Groves was greatly puzzled. Mrs Rumney's story, of course, was incredible, but this strange evil-faced man had appeared in the photograph somehow. That he had not been there when the print was made was quite certain.

The problem soon ceased to alarm Mr Groves; in his mind it was investing itself with a scientific interest. He began to think of suspended chemical action, and other possible avenues of investigation. At Mrs Rumney's urgent entreaty, however, he turned the photograph upon the easel, and with only its white back presented to the room, he sat down and ordered tea to be brought in.

He did not look again at the picture. The face of the man had about it something unnaturally painful: he could remember, and still see, as it were, the drawn features, and the look of the man had unaccountably distressed him.

He finished his slight meal, and having lit a pipe, began to brood over the scientific possibilities of the problem. Had any other photograph upon the original film become involved in the one he had enlarged? Had the image of any other face, distorted by the enlarging lens, become a part of this picture? For the space of two hours he debated this possibility, and that, only to reject them all. His optical knowledge told him that no conceivable accident could have brought into his picture a man with a roller.

No negative of his had ever contained such a man; if it had, no natural causes would suffice to leave him, as it were, hovering about the apparatus.

His repugnance to the actual thing had by this time lost its freshness, and he determined to end his scientific musings with another inspection of the object. So he approached the easel and turned the photograph round again. His horror returned, and with good cause. The man with the roller had now advanced to the middle of the lawn. The face was stricken still with the same indescribable look of suffering. The man seemed to be appealing to the spectator for some kind of help. Almost, he spoke.

Mr Groves was naturally reduced to a condition of extreme nervous excitement. Although not by nature what is called a nervous man, he trembled from head to foot. With a sudden effort, he turned away his head, took hold of the picture with his outstretched hand, and opening a drawer in his sideboard thrust the thing underneath a folded tablecloth which was lying there. Then he closed the drawer and took up an entertaining book to distract his thoughts from the whole matter.

In this he succeeded very ill. Yet somehow the rest of the evening passed, and as it wore away, he lost something of his alarm. At ten o'clock, Mrs Rumney, knocking and receiving answer twice, lest by any chance she should find herself alone in the room, brought in the cocoa usually taken by her lodger at that hour. A hasty glance at the easel showed her that it stood empty, and her face betrayed her relief. She made no comment, and Mr Groves invited none.

The latter, however, could not make up his mind to go to bed. The face he had seen was taking firm hold upon his imagination, and seemed to fascinate him and repel him at the same time. Before long, he found himself wholly unable to resist the impulse to look at it once more. He took it again, with some indecision, from the drawer and laid it under the lamp.

The man with the roller had now passed completely over the

lawn, and was near the left of the picture.

The shock to Mr Groves was again considerable. He stood facing the fire, trembling with excitement which refused to be suppressed. In this state his eye lighted upon the calendar hanging before him, and it furnished him with some distraction. The next day was his mother's birthday. Never did he omit to write a letter which should lie upon her breakfast-table, and the preoccupation of this evening had made him wholly forgetful of the matter. There was a collection of letters, however, from the pillar-box near at hand, at a quarter before midnight, so he turned to his desk, wrote a letter which would at least serve to convey his affectionate greetings, and having written it, went out into the night and posted it.

The clocks were striking midnight as he returned to his room. We may be sure that he did not resist the desire to glance at the photograph he had left on his table. But the results of that glance, he, at any rate, had not anticipated. The man with the roller had disappeared. The lawn lay as smooth and clear as at first, 'looking', as Mrs Rumney had said, 'as if it was waiting for someone to come and dance on it.'

The photograph, after this, remained a photograph and nothing more. Mr Groves would have liked to persuade himself that it had never undergone these changes which he had witnessed, and which we have endeavoured to describe, but his sense of their reality was too insistent. He kept the print lying for a week upon his easel. Mrs Rumney, although she had ceased to dread it, was obviously relieved at its disappearance, when it was carried to Stoneground to be delivered to Mr Batchel. Mr Groves said nothing of the man with the roller, but gave the enlargement, without comment, into his friend's hands. The work of enlargement had been skilfully done, and was deservedly praised.

Mr Groves, making some modest disclaimer, observed that the view, with its spacious foreground of lawn, was such as could not have failed to enlarge well. And this lawn, he added, as they sat looking out of the Vicar's study, looks as well from within your house as from without. It must give you a sense of responsibility, he added, reflectively, to be sitting where your predecessors have sat for so many centuries and to be continuing their peaceful work. The mere presence before your window, of the turf upon which good men have walked, is an inspiration.

The vicar made no reply to these somewhat sententious remarks. For a moment he seemed as if he would speak some words of conventional assent. Then he abruptly left the room, to return in a few minutes with a parchment book.

'Your remarks, Groves,' he said as he seated himself again, 'recalled to me a curious bit of history: I went up to the old library to get the book. This is the journal of William Longue who was vicar here up to the year 1602. What you said about the lawn will give you an interest in a certain portion of the journal. I will read it.'

Aug. 1, 1600—I am now returned in haste from a journey to Brightelmstone whither I had gone with full intention to remain about the space of two months. Master Josiah Wilburton, of my dear College of Emmanuel, having consented to assume the charge of my parish of Stoneground in the meantime. But I had intelligence, after 12 days' absence, by a messenger from the Churchwardens, that Master Wilburton had disappeared last Monday sennight, and had been no more seen. So here I am again in my study to the entire frustration of my plans, and can do nothing in my perplexity but sit and look out from my window, before which Andrew Birch rolleth the grass with much persistence. Andrew passeth so many times over the same place with his roller that I have just now stepped without to demand why he so wasteth his labour, and upon this he hath pointed out a place which is not levelled, and hath continued his rolling.

Aug. 2—There is a change in Andrew Birch since my absence, who hath indeed the aspect of one in great depression, which is noteworthy of so chearful a man. He haply shares our common trouble in respect of Master Wilburton, of whom we remain without tidings. Having made part of a sermon upon the seventh Chapter of the former Epistle of St. Paul to the Corinthians and the 27th verse, I found Andrew again at his task, and bade him desist and saddle my horse, being minded to ride forth and take counsel with my good friend John Palmer at the Deanery, who bore Master Wilburton great affection.

Aug. 2 continued—Dire news awaiteth me upon my return. The Sheriff's men have disinterred the body of poor Master W. from beneath the grass Andrew was rolling, and have arrested him on the charge of being his cause of death.

Aug. 10—Alas! Andrew Birch hath been hanged, the Justice having mercifully ordered that he should hang by the neck until he should be dead, and not sooner molested. May the Lord have mercy on his soul. He made full confession before me, that he had slain Master Wilburton in heat upon his threatening to make me privy to certain peculation of which I should not have suspected so old a servant. The poor man bemoaned his evil temper in great contrition, and beat his breast, saying that he knew himself doomed for ever to roll the grass in the place where he had tried to conceal his wicked fact.

'Thank you,' said Mr Groves. 'Has that little negative got the date upon it?' Yes, replied Mr Batchel, as he examined it with his glass. The boy has marked it August 10. The Vicar seemed not to remark the coincidence with the date of Birch's execution. Needless to say that it did not escape Mr Groves. But he kept silence about the man with the roller, who has been no more seen to this day.

Doubtless there is more in our photography than we yet know of. The camera sees more than the eye, and chemicals in a freshly prepared and active state, have a power which they afterwards lose. Our units of time, adopted for the convenience of persons dealing with the ordinary movements of material objects, are of course conventional. Those who turn the instruments of science upon nature will always be in danger of seeing more than they looked for. There is such a disaster as that of knowing too much, and at some time or another it may overtake each of us. May we then be as wise as Mr Groves in our reticence, if our turn should come.

BONE TO HIS BONE

WILLIAM WHITEHEAD, Fellow of Emmanuel College, in the University of Cambridge, became vicar of Stoneground in the year 1731. The annals of his incumbency were doubtless short and simple: they have not survived. In his day were no newspapers to collect gossip, no parish magazines to record the simple events of parochial life. One event, however, of greater moment then than now, is recorded in two places. Vicar Whitehead failed in health after 23 years of work, and journeyed to Bath in what his monument calls 'the vain hope of being restored'. The duration of his visit is unknown; it is reasonable to suppose that he made his journey in the summer, it is certain that by the month of November his physician told him to lay aside all hope of recovery.

Then it was that the thoughts of the patient turned to the comfortable straggling vicarage he had left at Stoneground, in which he had hoped to end his days. He prayed that his sucessor might be as happy there as he had been himself. Setting his affairs in order, as became one who had but a short time to live, he executed a will, bequeathing to the vicars of Stoneground, for ever, the close of ground he had recently purchased because it lay next to the vicarage garden. And by a codicil, he added to the bequest his library of books. Within a few days, William Whitehead was gathered to his fathers.

A mural tablet in the north aisle of the church, records, in Latin, his services and his bequests, his two marriages, and his fruitless journey to Bath. The house he loved, but never again saw, was taken down 40 years later, and rebuilt by vicar James Devie. The garden, with vicar Whitehead's 'close of ground' and other adjacent lands, was opened out and planted, somewhat before 1850, by vicar Robert Towerson. The aspect of everything has changed. But in a convenient chamber on the first floor of the present vicarage the library of vicar Whitehead stands very much as he used it and loved it, and as he bequeathed it to his successors 'for ever'.

The books there are arranged as he arranged and ticketed them. Little slips of paper, sometimes bearing interesting fragments of writing, still mark his places. His marginal comments still give life to pages from which all other interest has faded, and he would have but a dull imagination who could sit in the chamber amidst these books without ever being carried back 180 years into the past, to the time when the newest of them left the printer's hands.

Of those into whose possession the books have come, some have doubtless loved them more, and some less; some, perhaps, have left them severely alone. But neither those who loved them, not those who loved them not, have lost them, and they passed, some century and a half after William Whitehead's death, into the hands of Mr Batchel, who loved them as a father loves his children. He lived alone, and had few domestic cares to distract his mind. He was able, therefore, to enjoy to the full what vicar Whitehead had enjoyed so long before him. During many a long summer evening would he sit poring over long-forgotten books; and since the chamber, otherwise called the library, faced the south, he could also spend sunny winter mornings there without discomfort. Writing at a small table, or reading as he stood at a tall desk, he would browse amongst the books like an ox in a pleasant pasture.

There were other times also, at which Mr Batchel would use the books. Not being a sound sleeper (for book-loving men seldom are), he elected to use as a bedroom one of the two chambers which opened at either side into the library. The arrangement enabled him to beguile many a sleepless hour amongst the books, and in view of these nocturnal visits he kept a candle standing in a sconce above the desk, and matches always ready to his hand.

There was one disadvantage in this close proximity of his bed to the library. Owing, apparently, to some defect in the fittings of the room, which, having no mechanical tastes, Mr Batchel had never investigated, there could be heard, in the stillness of the night, exactly such sounds as might arise from a person moving about amongst the books. Visitors using the other adjacent room would often remark at breakfast, that they had heard their host in the library at one or two o'clock in the morning, when, in fact, he had not left his bed. Invariably Mr Batchel allowed them to suppose that he had been where they thought him. He disliked idle controversy, and was unwilling to afford an opening for supernatural talk. Knowing well enough the sounds by which his guests had been deceived, he wanted no other explanation of them than his own, though it was of too vague a character to count as an explanation. He conjectured that the window-sashes, or the doors, or 'something', were defective, and was too phlegmatic and too unpractical to make any investigation. The matter gave him no concern.

Persons whose sleep is uncertain are apt to have their worst nights when they would like their best. The consciousness of a special need for rest seems to bring enough mental disturbance to forbid it. So on Christmas Eve, in the year 1907, Mr Batchel, who would have liked to sleep well, in view of the labours of Christmas Day, lay hopelessly wide awake. He exhausted all the known devices for courting sleep, and, at the end, found himself wider than ever. A brilliant moon shone into his room, for he hated window-blinds. There was a light wind blowing, and the sounds in the library were more than usually suggestive of a person moving about. He almost determined to have the sashes 'seen to', although he could seldom be induced to have anything 'seen to'. He disliked changes, even for the better, and would submit to great inconvenience rather than have things altered with which he had become familiar.

As he revolved these matters in his mind, he heard the clocks strike the hour of midnight, and having now lost all hope of falling asleep, he rose from his bed, got into a large dressing gown which hung in readiness for such occasions, and passed into the library, with the intention of reading himself sleepy, if he could.

The moon, by this time, had passed out of the south, and the library seemed all the darker by contrast with the moonlit chamber he had left. He could see nothing but two blue-grey rectangles formed by the windows against the sky, the furniture of the room being altogether invisible. Groping along to where the table stood, Mr Batchel felt over its surface for the matches which usually lay there; he found, however, that the table was cleared of everything. He raised his right hand, therefore, in order to feel his way to a shelf where the matches were sometimes mislaid, and at that moment, whilst his hand was in mid-air, the matchbox was gently put into it!

Such an incident could hardly fail to disturb even a phlegmatic person, and Mr Batchel cried 'Who's this?' somewhat nervously. There was no answer. He struck a match, looked hastily round the room, and found it empty, as usual. There was everything, that is to say, that he was accustomed to see, but no other person than himself.

It is not quite accurate, however, to say that everything was in its usual state. Upon the tall desk lay a quarto volume that he had certainly not placed there. It was his quite invariable practice to replace his books upon the shelves after using them, and what we may call his library habits were precise and methodical. A book out of place like this, was not only an offence against good order, but a sign that his privacy had been intruded upon. With some surprise, therefore, he lit the candle standing ready in the sconce, and proceeded to examine the book, not sorry, in the disturbed condition in which he was, to have an occupation found for him.

The book proved to be one with which he was unfamiliar, and this made it certain that some other hand than his had removed it from its place. Its title was *The Compleat Gard'ner* of M. de la Quintinye made English by John Evelyn Esquire. It was not a work in which Mr Batchel felt any great interest. It consisted of diverse reflections on various parts of husbandry, doubtless entertaining enough, but too deliberate and discursive for practical purposes. He had certainly never used the book, and growing restless now in mind, said to himself that some boy having the freedom of the house, had taken it down from its place in the hope of finding pictures.

But even whilst he made this explanation he felt its weakness. To begin with, the desk was too high for a boy. The improbability that any boy would place a book there was equalled by the improbability that he would leave it there. To discover its uninviting character would be the work only of a moment, and no boy would have brought it so far from its shelf.

Mr Batchel had, however, come to read, and habit was too strong with him to be wholly set aside. Leaving *The Compleat Gard'ner* on the desk, he turned round to the shelves to find some more congenial reading.

Hardly had he done this when he was startled by a sharp rap upon the desk behind him, followed by a rustling of paper. He turned quickly about and saw the quarto lying open. In obedience to the instinct of the moment, he at once sought a natural cause for what he saw. Only a wind, and that of the strongest, could have opened the book, and laid back its heavy cover; and though he accepted, for a brief moment, that explanation, he was too candid to retain it longer. The wind out of doors was very light. The window sash was closed and latched, and, to decide the matter finally, the book had its back, and not its edges, turned towards the only quarter from which a wind could strike.

Mr Batchel approached the desk again and stood over the book. With increasing perturbation of mind (for he still thought of the matchbox) he looked upon the open page. Without much reason beyond that he felt constrained to do something, he read the words of the half completed sentence at the turn of the page:

at dead of night he left the house and passed into the solitude of the garden.

But he read no more, nor did he give himself the trouble of discovering whose midnight wandering was being described, although the habit was singularly like one of his own. He was in no condition for reading, and turning his back upon the volume he slowly paced the length of the chamber, 'wondering at that which had come to pass'.

He reached the opposite end of the chamber and was in the act of turning, when again he heard the rustling of paper, and by the time he had faced round, saw the leaves of the book again turning over. In a moment the volume lay at rest, open in another place, and there was no further movement as he approached it. To make sure that he had not been deceived, he read again the words as they entered the page. The author was following a not uncommon practise of the time, and throwing common speech into forms suggested by Holy Writ: 'So dig,' it said, 'that ye may obtain.'

This passage, which to Mr Batchel seemed reprehensible in its levity, excited at once his interest and his disapproval. He was prepared to read more, but this time was not allowed. Before his eye could pass beyond the passage already cited, the leaves of the book slowly turned again, and presented but a termination of five words and a colophon.

The words were, 'to the North, an Ilex'. These three passages, in which he saw no meaning and no connection, began to entangle themselves together in Mr Batchel's mind. He found himself repeating them in different orders, now beginning with one, and now with another. Any further attempt at reading he felt to be impossible, and he was in no mind for any more experiences of the unaccountable. Sleep was, of course, further from him than ever, if that were conceivable. What he did, therefore, was to blow out the candle, to return to his moonlit bedroom, and put on more clothing, and then to pass downstairs with the object of going out of doors.

It was not unusual with Mr Batchel to walk about his garden at night-time. This form of exercise had often, after a wakeful hour, sent him back to his bed refreshed and ready for sleep. The convenient access to the garden at such times lay through his study, whose French windows opened on to a short flight of steps, and upon these he now paused for a moment to admire the snow-like appearance of the lawns, bathed as they were in the moonlight. As he paused, he heard the city clocks strike the half-hour after midnight, and he could not forbear repeating aloud:

At dead of night he left the house, and passed into the solitude of the garden.

It was solitary enough. At intervals the screech of an owl, and now and then the noise of a train, seemed to emphasize the solitude by drawing attention to it and then leaving it in possession of the night. Mr Batchel found himself wondering and conjecturing what vicar Whitehead, who had acquired the close of land to secure quiet and privacy for garden, would have thought of the railways to the west and north. He turned his face northwards, whence a whistle had just sounded, and saw a tree beautifully outlined against the sky. His breath caught at the sight. Not because the tree was unfamiliar. Mr Batchel knew all his trees. But what he had seen was 'to the north, an Ilex'.

Mr Batchel knew not what to make of it all. He had walked into the garden hundreds of times and as often seen the Ilex, but the words out of *The Compleat Gard'ner* seemed to be pursuing him in a way that made him almost afraid. His temperament, however, as has been said already, was phlegmatic. It was commonly said, and Mr Batchel approved the verdict, whilst he condemned its inexactness, that 'his nerves were made of fiddle-string', so he braced himself afresh and set upon his walk round the silent garden, which he was accustomed to begin in a northerly direction, and was now too proud to change. He usually passed the Ilex at the beginning of his perambulation, and so would pass it now.

He did not pass it. A small discovery, as he reached it, annoyed and disturbed him. His gardener, as careful and punctilious as himself, never failed to house all his tools at the end of a day's work. Yet there, under the Ilex, standing upright in moonlight brilliant enough to cast a shadow of it, was a spade.

Mr Batchel's second thought was one of relief. After his extraordinary experiences in the library (he hardly knew now whether they had been real or not) something quite commonplace would act sedatively, and he determined to carry the spade to the tool-house.

The soil was quite dry, and the surface even a little frozen, so Mr Batchel left the path, walked up to the spade, and would have drawn it towards him. But it was as if he had made the attempt upon the trunk of the Ilex itself. The spade would not be moved. Then, first with one hand, and then with both, he tried to raise it, and still it stood firm. Mr Batchel, of course, attributed this to the frost, slight as it was. Wondering at the spade's being there, and annoyed at its being frozen, he was about to leave it and continue his walk, when the remaining words of *The Compleat Gard'ner* seemed rather to utter themselves, than to await his will:

So dig, that ye may obtain

Mr Batchel's power of independent action now deserted him. He took the spade, which no longer resisted, and began to dig. 'Five spadefuls and no more,' he said aloud. 'This is all foolishness.'

Four spadefuls of earth he then raised and spread out before him in the moonlight. There was nothing unusual to be seen. Nor did Mr Batchel decide what he would look for, whether coins, jewels, documents in canisters, or weapons. In point of fact, he dug against what he deemed his better judgement, and expected nothing. He spread before him the fifth and last spadeful of earth, not quite without result, but with no result that was at all sensational. The earth contained a bone. Mr Batchel's knowledge of anatomy was sufficient to show him that it was a human bone. He identified it, even by moonlight, as the radius, a bone of the forearm, as he removed the earth from it, with his thumb.

Such a discovery might be thought worthy of more than the very ordinary interest Mr Batchel showed. As a matter of fact, the presence of a human bone was easily to be accounted for. Recent excavations within the church had caused the upturning of numberless bones, which had been collected and reverently buried. But an earth-stained bone is also easily overlooked, and this radius had obviously found its way into the garden with some of the earth brought out of the church.

Mr Batchel was glad, rather than regretful at this termination to his adventure. He was once more provided with something to do. The re-interment of such bones as this had been his constant care, and he decided at once to restore the bone to consecrated earth. The time seemed opportune. The eyes of the curious were closed in sleep, he himself was still alert and wakeful. The spade remained by his side and the bone in his hand. So he betook himself, there and then, to the churchyard. By the still generous light of the moon, he found a place where the earth yielded to his spade, and within a few minutes the bone was laid decently to earth, some 18 inches deep.

The city clocks struck one as he finished. The whole world seemed asleep, and Mr Batchel slowly returned to the garden with his spade. As he hung it in its accustomed place he felt stealing over him the welcome desire to sleep. He walked quietly on to the house and ascended to his room. It was now dark: the moon had passed on and left the room in shadow. He lit a candle, and before undressing passed into the library. He had an irresistible curiosity to see the passages in John Evelyn's book which had so strangely adapted themselves to the events of the past hour.

In the library a last surprise awaited him. The desk upon which the book had lain was empty. *The Compleat Gard'ner* stood in its place on the shelf. And then Mr Batchel knew that he had handled a bone of William Whitehead, and that in response to his own entreaty.

THE RICHPINS

SOMETHING of the general character of Stoneground and its people has been indicated by stray allusions in the preceding narratives. We must here add that of its present population only a small part is native, the remainder having been attracted during the recent prosperous days of brickmaking, from the nearer parts of East Anglia and the Midlands. The visitor to Stoneground now finds little more than the signs of an unlovely industry, and of the hasty and inadequate housing of the people it has drawn together. Nothing in the place pleases him more than the excellent train service which makes it easy to get away. He seldom desires a long acquaintance either with Stoneground or its people.

The impression so made upon the average visitor is, however, unjust, as first impressions often are. The few who have made further acquaintance with Stoneground have soon learned to distinguish between the permanent and the accidental features of the place, and have been astonished by nothing so much as by the unexpected evidence of French influence. Amongst the household treasures of the old inhabitants are invariably found French knick-knacks: there are pieces of French furniture in what is called 'the room' of many houses. A certain ten-acre field is called the 'Frenchman's meadow'. Upon the voters' lists hanging at the church door are to be found French names, often corrupted; and boys who run about the streets can be heard shrieking to each other such names as Bunnum, Dangibow, Planchey, and so on.

Mr Batchel himself is possessed of many curious little articles of French handiwork—boxes deftly covered with split straws, arranged ingeniously in patterns; models of the guillotine, built of carved meat-bones, and various other pieces of handiwork, amongst them an accurate road-map of the country between Stoneground and Yarmouth, drawn upon a flyleaf torn from some book, and bearing upon the other side the name of Jules Richepin. The latter had been picked up, according to a pencilled note written across one corner, by a shepherd, in the year 1811.

The explanation of this French influence is simple enough. Within five miles of Stoneground a large barracks had been erected for the custody of French prisoners during the war with Bonaparte. Many thousands were confined there during the years 1808-14. The prisoners were allowed to sell what articles they could make in the barracks; and many of them, upon their release, settled in the neighbourhood, where their descendants remain. There is little curiosity amongst these descendants about their origin. The events of a century ago seem to them as remote as the Deluge, and as immaterial. To Thomas Richpin, a weakly man who blew the organ in church, Mr Batchel showed the map. Richpin, with a broad, blackhaired skull and a narrow chin which grew a little pointed beard, had always a foreign look about him: Mr Batchel thought it more than possible that he might be descended from the owner of the book, and told him as much upon showing him the flyleaf. Thomas, however, was content to observe that 'his name hadn't got no E', and showed no further interest in the matter. His interest in it, before we have done with him, will have become very large.

For the growing boys of Stoneground, with whom he was on generally friendly terms, Mr Batchel formed certain clubs to provide them with occupation on winter evenings; and in these clubs, in the interests of peace and good order, he spent a great deal of time. Sitting one December evening, in a large circle of boys who preferred the warmth of the fire to the more temperate atmosphere of the tables, he found Thomas Richpin the sole topic of conversation.

'We seen Mr Richpin in Frenchman's Meadow last night,' said one.

'What time?' said Mr Batchel, whose function it was to act as a sort of flywheel, and to carry the conversation over dead points. He had received the information with some little surprise, because Frenchman's Meadow was an unusual place for Richpin to have been in, but his question had no further object than to encourage talk.

'Half-past nine,' was the reply.

This made the question much more interesting. Mr Batchel, on the preceding evening, had taken advantage of a warmed church to practise upon the organ. He had played it from nine o'clock until ten, and Richpin had been all that time at the bellows.

'Are you sure it was half-past nine?' he asked.

'Yes,' (we reproduce the answer exactly), 'we come out o'night-school at quarter-past, and we was all goin' to the Wash to look if it was friz.'

'And you saw Mr Richpin in Frenchman's Meadow?' said Mr Batchel.

'Yes. He was looking for something on the ground,' added another boy.

'And his trousers was tore,' said a third.

The story was clearly destined to stand in no need of corroboration.

'Did Mr Richpin speak to you?' enquired Mr Batchel.

'No, we run away afore he come to us,' was the answer.

'Why?'

'Because we was frit.'

'What frightened you?'

'Jim Lallement hauled a flint at him and hit him in the face, and he didn't take no notice, so we run away.'

'Why?' repeated Mr Batchel.

'Because he never hollered nor looked at us, and it made us feel so funny.'

'Did you go straight down to the Wash?'

They had all done so.

'What time was it when you reached home?'

They had all been at home by ten, before Richpin had left the church.

'Why do they call it Frenchman's Meadow?' asked another boy, evidently anxious to change the subject.

Mr Batchel replied that the meadow had probably belonged to a Frenchman whose name was not easy to say, and the conversation after this was soon in another channel. But, furnished as he was with an unmistakable alibi, the story about Richpin and the torn trousers, and the flint, greatly puzzled him.

'Go straight home,' he said, as the boys at last bade him good-night, 'and let us have no more stone-throwing.' They were reckless boys, and Richpin, who used little discretion in reporting their misdemeanours about the church, seemed to Mr Batchel to stand in real danger.

Frenchman's Meadow provided ten acres of excellent pasture, and the owners of two or three hard-worked horses were glad to pay three shillings a week for the privilege of turning them into it. One of these men came to Mr Batchel on the morning which followed the conversation at the club.

'I'm in a bit of a quandary about Tom Richpin,' he began.

This was an opening that did not fail to command Mr Batchel's attention. 'What is it?' he said.

'I had my mare in Frenchman's Meadow,' replied the man, 'and Sam Bower come and told me last night as he heard her gallopin' about when he was walking this side the hedge.'

'But what about Richpin?' said Mr Batchel.

'Let me come to it,' said the other. 'My mare hasn't got no wind to gallop, so I up and went to see to her, and there she was sure enough, like a wild thing, and Tom Richpin walking across the meadow.'

'Was he chasing her?' asked Mr Batchel, who felt the absurdity of the question as he put it.

'He was not,' said the man, 'but what he could have been doin' to put the mare into that state, I can't think.'

'What was he doing when you saw him?' asked Mr Batchel.

'He was walking along looking for something he'd dropped, with his trousers all tore to ribbons, and while I was catchin' the mare, he made off.'

'He was easy enough to find, I suppose?' said Mr Batchel.

'That's the quandary I was put in,' said the man. 'I took the mare and gave her to my lad, and straight I went to Richpin's, and found Tom havin' his supper, with his trousers as good as new.'

'You'd made a mistake,' said Mr Batchel.

'But how come the mare to make it too?' said the other.

'What did you say to Richpin?' asked Mr Batchel.

' "Tom",' I says, "when did you come in?" "Six o'clock," he says, "I bin mendin' my boots"; and there, sure enough, was the hobbin' iron by his chair, and him in his stockin'-feet. I don't know what to do.'

'Give the mare a rest,' said Mr Batchel, 'and say no more about it.'

'I don't want to harm a pore creature like Richpin,' said the man, 'but a mare's a mare, especially where there's a family to bring up.' The man consented, however, to abide by Mr Batchel's advice, and the interview ended. The evenings just then were light, and both the man and his mare had seen something for which Mr Batchel could not, at present, account. The worst way, however, of arriving at an explanation is to guess it. He was far too wise to let himself wander into the pleasant fields of conjecture, and had determined, even before the story of the mare had finished, upon the more prosaic path of investigation.

Mr Batchel, either from strength or indolence of mind, as the reader may be pleased to determine, did not allow matters even of this exciting kind, to disturb his daily round of duty. He was beginning to fear, after what he had heard of the Frenchman's Meadow, that he might find it necessary to preach a plain sermon upon the Witch of Endor, for he foresaw that there would soon be some ghostly talk in circulation. In small communities, like that of Stoneground, such talk arises upon very slight provocation, and here was nothing at all to check it. Richpin was a weak and timid man, whom no one would suspect, whilst an alternative remained open, of wandering about in the dark; and Mr Batchel knew that the alternative of an apparition, if once suggested, would meet with general acceptance, and this he wished, at all costs, to avoid. His own view of the matter he held in reserve, for the reasons already stated, but he could not help suspecting that there might be a better explanation of the name 'Frenchman's Meadow' than he had given to the boys at their club.

Afternoons, with Mr Batchel, were always spent in making pastoral visits, and upon the day our story has reached he determined to include amongst them a call upon Richpin, and to submit him to a cautious cross-examination. It was evident that at least four persons, all perfectly familiar with his appearance, were under the impression that they had seen him in the meadow, and his own statement upon the matter would be at least worth hearing.

Richpin's home, however, was not the first one visited by Mr Batchel on that afternoon. His friendly relations with the boys has already been mentioned, and it may now be added that this friendship was but part of a generally keen sympathy with young people of all ages, and of both sexes. Parents knew much less than he did of the love affairs of their young people; and if he was not actually guilty of matchmaking, he was at least a very sympathetic observer of the process. When lovers had their little differences, or even their greater ones, it was Mr Batchel, in most cases, who adjusted them, and who suffered, if he failed, hardly less than the lovers themselves.

It was a negotiation of this kind which, on this particular day, had given precedence to another visit, and left Richpin until the later part of the afternoon. But the matter of the Frenchman's Meadow had, after all, not to wait for Richpin. Mr Batchel was calculating how long he should be in reaching it, when he found himself unexpectedly there. Selina Broughton had been a favourite of his from her childhood; she had been sufficiently good to please him, and naughty enough to attract and challenge him; and when at length she began to walk out with Bob Rockfort, who was another favourite, Mr Batchel rubbed his hands in satisfaction. Their present difference, which now brought him to the Broughtons' cottage, gave him but little anxiety. He had brought Bob half-way towards reconciliation, and had no doubt of his ability to lead Selina to the same place. They would finish the journey, happily enough, together.

But what has this to do with the Frenchman's Meadow? Much every way. The meadow was apt to be the rendezvous of such young people as desired a higher degree of privacy than that afforded by the public paths; and these two had gone there separately the night before, each to nurse a grievance against the other. They had been at opposite ends, as it chanced, of the field; and Bob, who believed himself to be alone there, had been awakened from his reverie by a sudden scream. He had at once run across the field, and found Selina sorely in need of him. Mr Batchel's work of reconciliation had been there and then anticipated, and Bob had taken the girl home in a condition of great excitement to her mother. All this was explained, in breathless sentences, by Mrs Broughton, by way of accounting for the fact that Selina was then lying down in 'the room'.

There was no reason why Mr Batchel should not see her, of course, and he went in. His original errand had lapsed, but it was now replaced by one of greater interest. Evidently there was Selina's testimony to add to that of the other four; she was not a girl who would scream without good cause, and Mr Batchel felt that he knew how his question about the cause would be answered, when he came to the point of asking it.

He was not quite prepared for the form of her answer, which she gave without any hesitation. She had seen Mr Richpin 'looking for his eyes'. Mr Batchel saved for another occasion the amusement to be derived from the curiously illogical answer. He saw at once what had suggested it. Richpin had until recently had an atrocious squint, which an operation in London had completely cured. This operation, of which, of course, he knew nothing, he had described, in his own way, to anyone who would listen, and it was commonly believed that his eyes had ceased to be fixtures. It was plain, however, that Selina had seen very much what had been seen by the other four. Her information was precise, and her story perfectly coherent. She preserved a maidenly reticence about his trousers, if she had noticed them; but added a new fact, and a terrible one, in her description of the eyeless sockets. No wonder she had screamed. It will be observed that Mr Richpin was still searching, if not looking, for something upon the ground.

Mr Batchel now proceeded to make his remaining visit. Richpin lived in a little cottage by the church, of which cottage the vicar was the indulgent landlord. Richpin's creditors were obliged to show some indulgence, because his income was never regular and seldom sufficient. He got on in life by what is called 'rubbing along', and appeared to do it with surprisingly little friction. The small duties about the church, assigned to him out of charity, were overpaid. He succeeded in attracting to himself all the available gifts of masculine clothing, of which he probably received enough and to sell, and he had somehow wooed and won a capable, if not very comely wife, who supplemented his income by her own labour, and managed her house and husband to admiration.

Richpin, however, was not by any means a mere dependant upon charity. He was, in his way, a man of parts. All plants, for instance, were his friends, and he had inherited, or acquired, great skill with fruit trees, which never failed to reward his treatment with abundant crops. The two or three vines, too, of the neighbourhood, he kept in fine order by methods of his own, whose merit was proved by their success. He had other skill, though of a less remunerative kind, in fashioning toys out of wood, cardboard, or paper; and every correctly behaving child in the parish had some such product of his handiwork. And besides all this, Richpin had a remarkable aptitude for making music. He could do something upon every musical instrument that came in his way, and, but for his voice, which was like that of the peahen, would have been a singer. It was his voice that had secured him the situation of organ-blower, as one remote from all incitement to join in the singing in church.

Like all men who have not wit enough to defend themselves by argument, Richpin had a plaintive manner. His way of resenting injury was to complain of it to the next person he met, and such complaints as he found no other means of discharging, he carried home to his wife, who treated his conversation just as she treated the singing of the canary, and other domestic sounds, being hardly conscious of it until it ceased.

The entrance of Mr Batchel, soon after his interview with Selina, found Richpin engaged in a loud and fluent oration. The fluency was achieved mainly by repetition, for the man had but small command of words, but it served none the less to show the depth of his indignation.

'I aren't bin in Frenchman's Meadow, am I?' he was saying in appeal to his wife—this is the Stoneground way with auxiliary verbs—'What am I got to go there for?' He acknowledged Mr Batchel's entrance in no other way than by changing to the third person in his discourse, and he continued without pause—'if she'd let me out o'nights, I'm got better places to go to than Frenchman's Meadow. Let policeman stick to where I am bin, or else keep his mouth shut. What call is he got to say I'm bin where I aren't bin?'

From this, and much more to the same effect, it was clear that the matter of the meadow was being noised abroad, and even receiving official attention. Mr Batchel was well aware that no question he could put to Richpin, in his present state, would change the flow of his eloquence, and that he had already learned as much as he was likely to learn. He was content, therefore, to ascertain from Mrs Richpin that her husband had indeed spent all his evenings at home, with the single exception of the one hour during which Mr Batchel had employed him at the organ. Having ascertained this, he retired, and left Richpin to talk himself out.

No further doubt about the story was now possible. It was not twenty-four hours since Mr Batchel had heard it from the boys at the club, and it had already been confirmed by at least two unimpeachable witnesses. He thought the matter over, as he took his tea, and was chiefly concerned in Richpin's curious connexion with it. On his account, more than on any other, it had become necessary to make whatever investigation might be feasible, and Mr Batchel determined, of course, to make the next stage of it in the meadow itself.

The situation of 'Frenchman's Meadow' made it more conspicuous than any other enclosure in the neighbourhood. It was upon the edge of what is locally known as 'high land'; and though its elevation was not great, one could stand in the meadow and look seawards over many miles of flat country, once a waste of brackish water, now a great chess-board of fertile fields bounded by straight dykes of glistening water. The point of view derived another interest from looking down upon a long straight bank which disappeared into the horizon many miles away, and might have been taken for a great railway embankment of which no use had been made. It was, in fact, one of the great works of the Dutch engineers in the time of Charles I, and it separated the river basin from a large drained area called the 'Middle Level', some six feet below it. In this embankment, not two hundred yards below 'Frenchman's Meadow', was one of the huge water gates which admitted traffic through a sluice, into the lower level, and the picturesque thatched cottage of the sluice-keeper formed a pleasing addition to the landscape. It was a view with which Mr Batchel was naturally very familiar. Few of his surroundings were pleasant to the eye, and this was about the only place to which he could take a visitor whom he desired to impress favourably. The way to the meadow lay through a short lane, and he could reach it in five minutes: he was frequently there.

It was, of course, his intention to be there again that evening: to spend the night there, if need be, rather than let anything escape him. He only hoped he should not find half the parish there also. His best hope of privacy lay in the inclemency of the weather; the day was growing colder, and there was a north-east wind, of which Frenchman's Meadow would receive the fine edge.

Mr Batchel spent the next three hours in dealing with some arrears of correspondence, and at nine o'clock put on his thickest coat and boots, and made his way to the meadow. It became evident, as he walked up the lane, that he was to have company. He heard many voices, and soon recognized the loudest amongst them. Jim Lallement was boasting of the accuracy of his aim: the others were not disputing it, but were asserting their own merits in discordant chorus. This was a nuisance, and to make matters worse, Mr Batchel heard steps behind him.

A voice soon bade him 'Good evening.' To Mr Batchel's great relief it proved to be the policeman, who soon overtook him. The conversation began on his side.

'Curious tricks, sir, these of Richpin's.'

'What tricks?' asked Mr Batchel, with an air of innocence.

'Why, he's been walking about Frenchman's Meadow these three nights, frightening folk and what all.'

'Richpin has been at home every night, and all night long,' said Mr Batchel.

'I'm talking about where he was, not where he says he was,' said the policeman. 'You can't go behind the evidence.'

'But Richpin has evidence too. I asked his wife.'

'You know, sir, and none better, that wives have got to obey. Richpin wants to be took for a ghost, and we know that sort of ghost. Whenever we hear there's a ghost, we always know there's going to be turkeys missing.'

'But there are real ghosts sometimes, surely?' said Mr Batchel.

'No,' said the policeman, 'me and my wife have both looked, and there's no such thing.'

'Looked where?' enquired Mr Batchel.

'In the "Police Duty" Catechism. There's lunatics, and deserters, and dead bodies, but no ghosts.'

Mr Batchel accepted this as final. He had devised a way of ridding himself of all his company, and proceeded at once to carry it into effect. The two had by this time reached the group of boys.

'These are all stone-throwers,' said he, loudly.

There was a clatter of stones as they dropped from the hands of the boys.

'These boys ought all to be in the club instead of roaming about here damaging property. Will you take them there, and see them safely in? If Richpin comes here, I will bring him to the station.'

The policeman seemed well pleased with the suggestion. No doubt he had overstated his confidence in the definition of the 'Police Duty'. Mr Batchel, on his part, knew the boys well enough to be assured that they would keep the policeman occupied for the next half-hour, and as the party moved slowly away, felt proud of his diplomacy.

There was no sign of any other person about the field gate, which he climbed readily enough, and he was soon standing in the highest part of the meadow and peering into the darkness on every side.

It was possible to see a distance of about thirty yards; beyond that it was too dark to distinguish anything. Mr Batchel designed a zigzag course about the meadow, which would allow of his examining it systematically and as rapidly as possible, and along this course he began to walk briskly, looking straight before him as he went, and pausing to look well about him when he came to a turn. There were no beasts in the meadow—their owners had taken the precaution of removing them; their absence was, of course, of great advantage to Mr Batchel.

In about ten minutes he had finished his zigzag path and arrived at the other corner of the meadow; he had seen nothing resembling a man. He then retraced his steps, and examined the field again, but arrived at his starting point, knowing no more than when he had left it. He began to fear the return of the policeman as he faced the wind and set upon a third journey.

The third journey, however, rewarded him. He had reached the end of his second traverse, and was looking about him at the angle between that and the next, when he distinctly saw what looked like Richpin crossing his circle of vision, and making straight for the sluice. There was no gate on that side of the field; the hedge, which seemed to present no obstacle to the other, delayed Mr Batchel considerably, and still retains some of his clothing, but he was not long through before he had again marked his man. It had every appearance of being Richpin. It went down the slope, crossed the plank that bridged the lock, and disappeared round the corner of the cottage, where the entrance lay.

Mr Batchel had had no opportunity of confirming the gruesome observation of Selina Broughton, but had seen enough to prove that the others had not been romancing. He was not a half-minute behind the figure as it crossed the plank over the lock—it was slow going in the darkness—and he followed it immediately round the corner of the house. As he expected, it had then disappeared.

Mr Batchel knocked at the door, and admitted himself, as his custom was. The sluice-keeper was in his kitchen, charring a gate post. He was surprised to see Mr Batchel at that hour, and his greeting took the form of a remark to that effect.

'I have been taking an evening walk,' said Mr Batchel. 'Have you seen Richpin lately?'

'I see him last Saturday week,' replied the sluice-keeper, 'not since.'

'Do you feel lonely here at night?'

'No,' replied the sluice-keeper, 'people drop in at times. There was a man in on Monday, and another yesterday.'

'Have you had no one today?' said Mr Batchel, coming to the point.

The answer showed that Mr Batchel had been the first to enter the door that day, and after a little general conversation he brought his visit to an end.

It was now ten o'clock. He looked in at Richpin's cottage, where he saw a light burning, as he passed. Richpin had tired himself early, and had been in bed since half-past eight. His wife was visibly annoyed at the rumours which had upset him, and Mr Batchel said such soothing words as he could command, before he left for home.

He congratulated himself, prematurely, as he sat before the fire in his study, that the day was at an end. It had been cold out of doors, and it was pleasant to think things over in the warmth of the cheerful fire his housekeeper never failed to leave for him. The reader will have no more difficulty than Mr Batchel had in accounting for the resemblance between Richpin and the man in the meadow. It was a mere question of family likeness. That the ancestor had been seen in the meadow at some former time might perhaps be inferred from its traditional name. The reason for his return, then and now, was a matter of mere conjecture, and Mr Batchel let it alone.

The next incident has, to some, appeared incredible, which only means, after all, that it has made demands upon their powers of imagination and found them bankrupt.

Critics of story-telling have used severe language about authors who avail themselves of the short-cut of coincidence. 'That must be reserved, I suppose,' said Mr Batchel, when he came to tell of Richpin, 'for what really happens; and that fiction is a game which must be played according to the rules.'

'I know,' he went on to say, 'that the chances were some millions to one against what happened that night, but if that makes it incredible, what is there left to believe?'

It was thereupon remarked by someone in the company, that the credible material would not be exhausted.

'I doubt whether anything happens,' replied Mr Batchel in his dogmatic way, 'without the chances being a million to one against it. Why did they choose such a word? What does "happen" mean?'

There was no reply: it was clearly a rhetorical question.

'Is it incredible,' he went on, 'that I put into the plate last Sunday the very half-crown my uncle tipped me with in 1881, and that I spent next day?'

'Was that the one you put in?' was asked by several.

'How do I know?' replied Mr Batchel, 'but if I knew the history of the half-crown I did put in, I know it would furnish still more remarkable coincidences.'

All this talk arose out of the fact that at midnight on the eventful day, whilst Mr Batchel was still sitting by his study fire, he had news that the cottage at the sluice had been burnt down. The thatch had been dry; there was, as we know, a stiff east wind, and an hour had sufficed to destroy all that was inflammable. The fire is still spoken of in Stoneground with great regret. There remains only one building in the place of sufficient merit to find its way on to a postcard.

It was just at midnight that the sluice-keeper rung at Mr Batchel's door. His errand required no apology. The man had found a night-fisherman to help him as soon as the fire began, and with two long sprits from a lighter they had made haste to tear down the thatch, and upon this had brought down, from under the ridge at the South end, the bones and some of the clothing of a man. Would Mr Batchel come down and see?

Mr Batchel put on his coat and returned to the place. The people whom the fire had collected had been kept on the further side of the water, and the space about the cottage was vacant. Near to the smouldering heap of ruin were the remains found under the thatch. The fingers of the right hand still firmly clutched a sheep bone which had been gnawed as a dog would gnaw it.

'Starved to death,' said the sluice-keeper, 'I see a tramp like that ten years ago.'

They laid the bones decently in an outhouse, and turned the key. Mr Batchel carried home in his hand a metal cross, threaded upon a cord. He found an engraved figure of Our Lord on the face of it, and the name of Pierre Richepin upon the back. He went next day to make the matter known to the nearest priest of the Roman Faith, with whom he left the cross. The remains, after a brief inquest, were interred in the cemetery, with the rites of the Church to which the man had evidently belonged.

Mr Batchel's deductions from the whole circumstances were curious, and left a great deal to be explained. It seemed as if Pierre Richepin had been disturbed by some premonition of the fire, but had not foreseen that his mortal remains would escape; that he could not return to his own people without the aid of his map, but had no perception of the interval that had elapsed since he had lost it. This map Mr Batchel put into his pocket-book next day when he went to Thomas Richpin for certain other information about his surviving relatives.

Richpin had a father, it appeared, living a few miles away in

Jakesley Fen, and Mr Batchel concluded that he was worth a visit. He mounted his bicycle, therefore, and made his way to Jakesley that same afternoon.

Mr Richpin was working not far from home, and was soon brought in. He and his wife showed great courtesy to their visitor, whom they knew well by repute. They had a well-ordered house, and with a natural and dignified hospitality, asked him to take tea with them. It was evident to Mr Batchel that there was a great gulf between the elder Richpin and his son; the former was the last of an old race, and the latter the first of a new. In spite of the Board of Education, the latter was vastly the worse.

The cottage contained some French kickshaws which greatly facilitated the enquiries Mr Batchel had come to make. They proved to be family relics.

'My grandfather,' said Mr Richpin, as they sat at tea, 'was a prisoner—he and his brother.'

'Your grandfather was Pierre Richepin?' asked Mr Batchel.

'No! Jules,' was the reply. 'Pierre got away.'

'Show Mr Batchel the book,' said his wife.

The book was produced. It was a Book of Meditations, with the name of Jules Richepin upon the title-page. The flyleaf was missing. Mr Batchel produced the map from his pocketbook. It fitted exactly. The slight indentures along the torn edge fell into their place, and Mr Batchel left the leaf in the book, to the great delight of the old couple, to whom he told no more of the story than he thought fit.

THE EASTERN WINDOW

It may well be that Vermuyden and the Dutchmen who drained the fens did good, and that it was interred with their bones. It is quite certain that they did evil and that it lives after them. The rivers, which these men robbed of their water, have at length silted up, and the drainage of one tract of country is proving to have been achieved by the undraining of another.

Places like Stoneground, which lie on the banks of these defrauded rivers, are now become helpless victims of Dutch engineering. The water which has lost its natural outlet, invades their lands. The thrifty cottager who once had the river at the bottom of his garden, has his garden more often in these days, at the bottom of the river, and a summer flood not infrequently destroys the whole produce of his ground.

Such a flood, during an early year in the twentieth century, had been unusually disastrous to Stoneground, and Mr Batchel, who, as a gardener, was well able to estimate the losses of his poorer neighbours, was taking some steps towards repairing them.

Money, however, is never at rest in Stoneground, and it turned out upon this occasion that the funds placed at his command were wholly inadequate to the charitable purpose assigned to them. It seemed as if those who had lost a rood of potatoes could be compensated for no more than a yard.

It was at this time, when he was oppressed in mind by the

failure of his charitable enterprise, that Mr Batchel met with the happy adventure in which the Eastern window of the church played so singular a part.

The narrative should be prefaced by a brief description of the window in question. It is a large painted window, of a somewhat unfortunate period of execution. The drawing and colouring leave everything to be desired. The scheme of the window, however, is based upon a wholesome tradition. The five large lights in the lower part are assigned to five scenes in the life of Our Lord, and the second of these, counting from the north, contains a bold erect figure of St John the Baptist, to whom the church is dedicated. It is this figure alone, of all those contained in the window, that is concerned in what we have to relate.

It has already been mentioned that Mr Batchel had some knowledge of music. He took an interest in the choir, from whose practices he was seldom absent; and was quite competent, in the occasional absence of the choirmaster, to act as his deputy. It is customary at Stoneground for the choirmaster, in order to save the sexton a journey, to extinguish the lights after a choir-practice and to lock up the church. These duties, accordingly, were performed by Mr Batchel when the need arose.

It will be of use to the reader to have the procedure in detail. The large gas-meter stood in an aisle of the church, and it was Mr Batchel's practice to go round and extinguish all the lights save one, before turning off the gas at the meter. The one remaining light, which was reached by standing upon a choir seat, was always that nearest the door of the chancel, and experience proved that there was ample time to walk from the meter to that light before it died out. It was therefore an easy matter to turn off the last light, to find the door without its aid, and thence to pass out, and close the church for the night.

Upon the evening of which we have to speak, the choir had hurried out as usual, as soon as the word had been given. Mr Batchel had remained to gather together some of the books they had left in disorder, and then turned out the lights in the manner already described. But as soon as he had extinguished the last light, his eye fell, as he descended carefully from the seat, upon the figure of the Baptist. There was just enough light outside to make the figures visible in the eastern window, and Mr Batchel saw the figure of St John raise the right arm to its full extent, and point northward, turning its head, at the same time, so as to look him full in the face. These movements were three times repeated, and, after that, the figure came to rest in its normal and familiar position.

The reader will not suppose, any more than Mr Batchel supposed, that a figure painted upon glass had suddenly been endowed with the power of movement. But that there had been the appearance of movement admitted of no doubt, and Mr Batchel was not so incurious as to let the matter pass without some attempt at investigation. It must be remembered, too, that an experience in the old library, which has been previously recorded, had pre-disposed him to give attention to signs which another man might have wished to explain away. He was not willing, therefore, to leave this matter where it stood. He was quite prepared to think that his eye had been deceived, but was none the less determined to find out what had deceived it. One thing he had no difficulty in deciding. If the movement had not been actually within the Baptist's figure, it had been immediately behind it. Without delay, therefore, he passed out of the church and locked the door after him, with the intention of examining the other side of the window.

Every inhabitant of Stoneground knows, and laments, the ruin of the old Manor House. Its loss by fire some fifteen years ago was a calamity from which the parish has never recovered. The estate was acquired, soon after the destruction of the house, by speculators who have been unable to turn it to any account, and it has for a decade or longer been 'let alone', except by the forces of nature and the wantonness of trespassers. The charred remains of the house still project above the surrounding heaps of fallen masonry, which have long been overgrown by such vegetation as thrives on neglected ground; and what was once a stately house, with its garden and park in fine order, has given place to a scene of desolation and ruin.

Stoneground church was built, some 600 years ago, within the enclosure of the Manor House, or, as it was anciently termed, the Burystead, and an excellent stratum of gravel such as no builder would wisely disregard brought the house and church unusually near together. In more primitive days, the nearness probably caused no inconvenience; but when change and progress affected the popular idea of respectful distance, the churchyard came to be separated by a substantial stone wall, of sufficient height to secure the privacy of the house.

The change was made with necessary regard to economy of space. The eastern wall of the church already projected far into the garden of the Manor, and lay but fifty yards from the south front of the house. On that side of the churchyard, therefore, the new wall was set back. Running from the north to the nearest corner of the church, it was there built up to the church itself, and then continued from the southern corner, leaving the eastern wall and window within the garden of the squire. It was his ivy that clung to the wall of the church, and his trees that shaded the window from the morning sun.

Whilst we have been recalling these facts, Mr Batchel has made his way out of the church and through the churchyard, and has arrived at a small door in the boundary wall, close to the south-east corner of the chancel. It was a door which some squire of the previous century had made, to give convenient access to the church for himself and his household. It has no present use, and Mr Batchel had some difficulty in getting it open. It was not long, however, before he stood on the innder side, and was examining the second light of the window. There was a tolerably bright moon, and the dark surface of the glass could be distinctly seen, as well as the wirework placed there for its protection.

A tall birch, one of the trees of the old churchyard, had thrust its lower boughs across the window, and their silvery bark shone in the moonlight. The boughs were bare of leaves, and only very slightly interrupted Mr Batchel's view of the Baptist's figure, the leaden outline of which was clearly traceable. There was nothing, however, to account for the movement which Mr Batchel was curious to investigate.

He was about to turn homewards in some disappointment, when a cloud obscured the moon again, and reduced the light to what it had been before he left the church. Mr Batchel watched the darkening of the window and the objects near it, and as the figure of the Baptist disappeared from view there came into sight a creamy vaporous figure of another person lightly poised upon the bough of the tree, and almost coincident in position with the picture of the Saint.

It could hardly be described as the figure of a person. It had more the appearance of half a person, and fancifully suggested to Mr Batchel, who was fond of whist, one of the diagonally bisected knaves in a pack of cards, as he appears when another card conceals a triangular half of the bust.

There was no question, now, of going home. Mr Batchel's eyes were riveted upon the apparition. It disappeared again for a moment, when an interval between two clouds restored the light of the moon; but no sooner had the second cloud replaced the first than the figure again became distinct. And upon this, its single arm was raised three times, pointing northwards towards the ruined house, just as the figure of the Baptist had seemed to point when Mr Batchel had seen it from within the church.

It was natural that upon receipt of this sign Mr Batchel should step nearer to the tree, from which he was still at some little distance, and as he moved, the figure floated obliquely downwards and came to rest in a direct line between him and the ruins of the house. It rested, not upon the ground, but in just such a position as it would have occupied if the lower parts had been there, and in this position it seemed to await Mr Batchel's advance. He made such haste to approach it as was possible upon ground encumbered with ivy and brambles, and the figure responded to every advance of his by moving further in the direction of the ruin.

As the ground improved, the progress became more rapid. Soon they were both upon an open stretch of grass, which in better days had been a lawn, and still the figure retreated towards the building, with Mr Batchel in respectful pursuit. He saw it, at last, poised upon the summit of a heap of masonry, and it disappeared, at his near approach, into a crevice between two large stones.

The timely re-appearance of the moon just enabled Mr Batchel to perceive this crevice, and he took advantage of the interval of light to mark the place. Taking up a large twig that lay at his feet, he inserted it between the stones. He made a slit in the free end and drew into it one of some papers that he had carried out of the Church. After such a precaution it could hardly be possible to lose the place—for, of course, Mr Batchel intended to return in daylight and continue his investigation. For the present, it seemed to be at an end. The light was soon obscured again, but there was no reappearance of the singular figure he had followed, so after remaining about the spot for a few minutes, Mr Batchel went home to his customary occupation.

He was not a man to let these occupations be disturbed even by a somewhat exciting adventure, nor was he one of those who regard an unusual experience only as a sign of nervous disorder. Mr Batchel had far too broad a mind to discredit his sensations because they were not like those of other people. Even had his adventure of the evening been shared by some companion who saw less than he did, Mr Batchel would only have inferred that his own part in the matter was being regarded as more important.

Next morning, therefore, he lost no time in returning to the scene of his adventure. He found his mark undisturbed, and was able to examine the crevice into which the apparition had seemed to enter. It was a crevice formed by the curved surfaces of two large stones which lay together on the top of a small heap of fallen rubbish, and these two stones Mr Batchel proceeded to remove. His strength was just sufficient for the purpose. He laid the stones upon the ground on either side of the little mound, and then proceeded to remove, with his hands, the rubbish upon which they had rested, and amongst the rubbish he found, tarnished and blackened, two silver coins.

It was not a discovery which seemed to afford any explanation of what had occurred the night before, but Mr Batchel could not but suppose that there had been an attempt to direct his attention to the coins, and he carried them away with a view of submitting them to a careful examination. Taking them up to his bedroom he poured a little water into a hand basin, and soon succeeded, with the aid of soap and a nail brush, in making them tolerably clean. Ten minutes later, after adding ammonia to the water, he had made them bright, and after carefully drying them, was able to make his examination. They were two crowns of the time of Queen Anne, minted, as a small letter E indicated, at Edinburgh, and stamped with the roses and plumes which testified to the English and Welsh silver in their composition. The coins bore no date, but Mr Batchel had no hesitation in assigning them to the year 1708 or thereabouts. They were handsome coins, and in themselves a find of considerable interest, but there was nothing to show why he had been directed to their place of concealment. It was an enigma, and he could not solve it. He had other work to do, so he laid the two crowns upon his dressing table, and proceeded to do it.

Mr Batchel thought little more of the coins until bedtime, when he took them from the table and bestowed upon them another admiring examination by the light of his candle. But the examination told him nothing new: he laid them down again, and, before very long, had lain his own head upon the pillow.

It was Mr Batchel's custom to read himself to sleep. At this time he happened to be re-reading the Waverley novels, and *Woodstock* lay upon the reading-stand which was always placed at his bedside. As he read of the cleverly devised apparition at Woodstock, he naturally asked himself whether he might not have been the victim of some similar trickery, but was not long in coming to the conclusion that his experience admitted of no such explanation. He soon dismissed the matter from his mind and went on with his book.

On this occasion, however, he was tired of reading before he was ready for sleep; it was long in coming, and then did not come to stay. His rest, in fact, was greatly disturbed. Again and again, perhaps every hour or so, he was awakened by an uneasy consciousness of some other presence in the room.

Upon one of his later awakenings, he was distinctly sensible of a sound, or what he described to himself as the 'ghost' of a sound. He compared it to the whining of a dog that had lost its voice. It was not a very intelligible comparison, but still it seemed to describe his sensation. The sound, if we may so call it caused him first to sit up in bed and look well about him, and then, when nothing had come of that, to light his candle. It was not to be expected that anything should come of that, but it had seemed a comfortable thing to do, and Mr Batchel left the candle alight and read his book for half an hour or so, before blowing it out.

After this, there was no further interruption, but Mr Batchel distinctly felt, when it was time to leave his bed, that he had had a bad night. The coins, almost to his surprise, lay undisturbed. He went to ascertain this as soon as he was on his feet. He would almost have welcomed their removal, or at any rate, some change which might have helped him towards a theory of his adventure. There was, however, nothing. If he had, in fact, been visited during the night, the coins would seem to have had nothing to do with the matter.

Mr Batchel left the two crowns lying on his table on this next day, and went about his ordinary duties. They were such duties as afforded full occupation for his mind, and he gave no more than a passing thought to the coins, until he was again retiring to rest. He had certainly intended to return to the heap of rubbish from which he had taken them, but had not found leisure to do so. He did not handle the coins again. As he undressed, he made some attempt to estimate their value, but without having arrived at any conclusion, went on to think of other things, and in a little while had lain down to rest again, hoping for a better night.

His hopes were disappointed. Within an hour of falling asleep he found himself awakened again by the voiceless whining he so well remembered. This sound, as for convenience we will call it, was now persistent and continuous. Mr Batchel gave up even trying to sleep, and as he grew more restless and uneasy, decided to get up and dress.

It was the entire cessation of the sound at this juncture which led him to a suspicion. His rising was evidently giving satisfaction. From that it was easy to infer that something had been desired of him, both on the present and the preceding night. Mr Batchel was not one to hold himself aloof in such a case. If help was wanted, even in such unnatural circumstances, he was ready to offer it. He determined, accordingly, to return to the Manor House, and when he had finished dressing, descended the stairs, put on a warm overcoat and went out, closing his hall door behind him, without having heard any more of the sound, either whilst dressing, or whilst leaving the house.

Once out of doors, the suspicion he had formed was strengthened into a conviction. There was no manner of doubt that he had been fetched from his bed; for about 30 yards in front of him he saw the strange creamy half-figure making straight for the ruins. He followed it as well as he could; as before, he was impeded by the ivy and weeds, and the figure awaited him; as before, it made straight for the heap of masonry and disappeared as soon as Mr Batchel was at liberty to follow.

There were no dungeons, or subterranean premises beneath the Manor House. It had never been more than a house of residence, and the building had been purely domestic in character. Mr Batchel was convinced that his adventure would prove unromantic, and felt some impatience at losing again, what he had begun to call his triangular friend. If this friend wanted anything, it was not easy to say why he had so tamely disappeared. There seemed nothing to be done but to wait until he came out again.

Mr Batchel had a pipe in his pocket, and he seated himself upon the base of a sundial within full view of the spot. He filled and smoked his pipe, sitting in momentary expectation of some further sign, but nothing appeared. He heard the hedgehogs moving about him in the undergrowth, and now and then the sound of a restless bird overhead, otherwise all was still. He smoked a second pipe without any further discovery, and that finished, he knocked out the ashes against his boot, walked to the mound, near to which his labelled stick was lying, thrust the stick into the place where the figure had disappeared, and went back to bed, where he was rewarded with five hours of sound sleep.

Mr Batchel had made up his mind that the next day ought to be a day of disclosure. He was early at the Manor House, this time provided with the gardener's pick, and a spade. He thrust the pick into the place from which he had removed his mark, and loosened the rubbish thoroughly. With his hands, and with his spade, he was not long in reducing the size of the heap, by about one-half, and there he found more coins.

There were three more crowns, two half-crowns, and a dozen or so of smaller coins. All these Mr Batchel wrapped carefully in his handkerchief, and after a few minutes' rest went on with his task. As it proved, the task was nearly over. Some strips of oak about nine inches long, were next uncovered, and then, what Mr Batchel had begun to expect, the lid of a box, with the hinges still attached. It lay, face downwards, upon a flat stone. It proved, when he had taken it up, to be almost unsoiled, and above a long and wide slit in the lid was the gilded legend, 'for ye poore' in the graceful lettering and the redundant spelling of two centuries ago.

The meaning of all this Mr Batchel was not long in interpreting. That the box and its contents had fallen and been broken amongst the masonry, was evident enough. It was as evident that it had been concealed in one of the walls brought down by the fire, and Mr Batchel had no doubt at all that he had been in the company of a thief, who had once stolen the poor-box from the church. His task seemed to be at an end, a further rummage revealed nothing new. Mr Batchel carefully collected the fragments of the box, and left the place.

His next act cannot be defended. He must have been aware that these coins were 'treasure trove', and therefore the property of the Crown. In spite of this, he determined to convert them into current coin, as he well knew how, and to apply the proceeds to the Inundation Fund about which he was so anxious. Treating them as his own property, he cleaned them all, as he had cleaned the two crowns, sent them to an antiquarian friend in London to sell for him, and awaited the result. The lid of the poor-box he still preserves as a relic of the adventure.

His antiquarian friend did not keep him long waiting. The coins had been eagerly bought, and the price surpassed any expectation that Mr Batchel had allowed himself to entertain. He had sent the package to London on Saturday morning. Upon the following Tuesday, the last post in the evening brought a cheque for twenty guineas. The brief subscription list of the Inundation Fund lay upon his desk, and he at once entered the amount he had so strangely come by, but could not immediately decide upon its description. Leaving the line blank, therefore, he merely wrote down £21 in the cash column, to be assigned to its source in some suitable form of words when he should have found time to frame them.

In this state he left the subscription list upon his desk, when he retired for the night. It occurred to him as he was undressing, that the twenty guineas might suitably be described as a 'restitution', and so he determined to enter it upon the line he had left vacant. As he reconsidered the matter in the morning, he saw no reason to alter his decision, and he went straight from his bedroom to his desk to make the entry and have done with it.

There was an incident in the adventure, however, upon which Mr Batchel had not reckoned. As he approached the list, he saw, to his amazement, that the line had been filled in. In a crabbed, elongated hand was written, 'At last, St Matt v 26.'

What may seem more strange is that the handwriting was familiar to Mr Batchel, he could not at first say why. His memory, however, in such matters, was singularly good, and before breakfast was over he felt sure of having identified the writer.

His confidence was not misplaced. He went to the parish chest, whose contents he had thoroughly examined in past intervals of leisure, and took out the roll of parish constable's accounts. In a few minutes he discovered the handwriting of which he was in search. It was unmistakably that of Salathiel Thrapston, constable from 1705-1710, who met his death in the latter year, whilst in the execution of his duty. The reader will scarcely need to be reminded of the text of the Gospel at the place of reference:

'Thou shalt by no means come out thence till thou hast paid the uttermost farthing.'

LUBRIETTA

FOR the better understanding of this narrative we shall furnish the reader with a few words of introduction. It amounts to no more than a brief statement of facts which Mr Batchel obtained from the Lady Principal of the European College in Puna, but the facts nevertheless are important. The narrative itself was obtained from Mr Batchel with difficulty: he was disposed to regard it as unsuitable for publication because of the delicate nature of the situations with which it deals. When, however, it was made clear to him that it would be recorded in such a manner as would interest only a very select body of readers, his scruples were overcome, and he was induced to communicate the experience now to be related. Those who read it will not fail to see that they are in a manner pledged to deal very discreetly with the knowledge they are privileged to share.

Lubrietta Rodria is described by her Lady Principal as an attractive and high-spirited girl of seventeen, belonging to the Purple of Indian commerce. Her nationality was not precisely known; but drawing near, as she did, to a marriageable age, and being courted by more than one eligible suitor, she was naturally an object of great interest to her schoolfellows, with whom her personal beauty and amiable temper had always made her a favourite. She was not, the Lady Principal thought, a girl who would be regarded in Christian countries as of very high principle; but none the less, she was one whom it was impossible not to like.

Her career at the college had ended sensationally. She had been immoderately anxious about her final examination, and its termination had found her in a state of collapse. They had at once removed her to her father's house in the country, where she received such nursing and assiduous attention as her case required. It was apparently of no avail. For three weeks she lay motionless, deprived of speech, and voluntarily, taking no food. Then for a further period of ten days she lay in a plight still more distressing. She lost all consciousness, and, despite the assurance of the doctors, her parents could hardly be persuaded that she lived.

Her fiance who by this time had been declared, was in despair, not only from natural affection for Lubrietta, but from remorse. It was his intellectual ambition that had incited her to the eagerness in study which was threatening such dire results, and it was well understood that neither of the lovers would survive these anxious days of watching if they were not to be survived by both.

After ten days, however, a change supervened. Lubrietta came back to life amid the frenzied rejoicing of the household and all her circle. She recovered her health and strength with incredible speed, and within three months was married—as the Lady Principal had cause to believe, with the happiest prospects.

Mr Batchel had not, whilst residing at Stoneground, lost touch with the university which had given him his degree, and in which he had formerly held one or two minor offices. He had earned no great distinction as a scholar, but had taken a degree in honours, and was possessed of a useful amount of general knowledge, and in this he found not only constant pleasure, but also occasional profit.

The university had made herself, for better or worse, an examiner of a hundred times as many students as she could teach;

her system of examinations had extended to the very limits of the British Empire, and her certificates of proficiency were coveted in every quarter of the globe.

In the examination of these students, Mr Batchel, who had considerable experience in teaching, was annually employed. Papers from all parts of the world were to be found littered about his study, and the examination of these papers called for some weeks of strenuous labour at every year's end. As the weeks passed, he would anxiously watch the growth of a neat stack of papers in the corner of the room, which indicated the number to which marks had been assigned and reported to Cambridge. The day upon which the last of these was laid in its place was a day of satisfaction, second only to that which later on brought him a substantial cheque to remunerate him for his labours.

During this period of special effort, Mr Batchel's servants had their share of its discomforts. The chairs and tables they wanted to dust and to arrange, were loaded with papers which they were forbidden to touch; and although they were warned against showing visitors into any room where these papers were lying, Mr Batchel would inconsiderately lay them in every room he had. The privacy of his study, however, where the work was chiefly done, was strictly guarded, and no one was admitted there unless by Mr Batchel himself.

Imagine his annoyance, therefore, when he returned from an evening engagement at the beginning of the month of January, and found a stranger seated in the study! Yet the annoyance was not long in subsiding. The visitor was a lady, and as she sat by the lamp, a glance was enough to show that she was young, and very beautiful. The interest which this young lady excited in Mr Batchel was altogether unusual, as unusual as was the visit of such a person at such a time. His conjecture was that she had called to give him notice of a marriage, but he was really charmed by her presence, and was quite content to find her in no haste to state her errand. The manner, however, of the lady was singular, for neither by word nor movement did she show that she was conscious of Mr Batchel's entry into the room.

He began at length with his customary formula 'What can I have the pleasure of doing for you?' and when, at the sound of his voice, she turned her fine dark eyes upon him, he saw that they were wet with tears.

Mr Batchel was now really moved. As a tear fell upon the lady's cheek, she raised her hand as if to conceal it—a brilliant sapphire sparkling in the lamplight as she did so. And then the lady's distress, and the exquisite grace of her presence, altogether overcame him. There stole upon him a strange feeling of tenderness which he supposed to be paternal, but knew nevertheless to be indiscreet. He was a prudent man, with strict notions of propriety, so that, ostensibly with a view to giving the lady a few minutes in which to recover her composure, he quietly left the study and went into another room, to pull himself together.

Mr Batchel, like most solitary men, had a habit of talking to himself. 'It is of no use, R.B.,' he said, 'to pretend that you have retired on this damsel's account. If you don't take care, you'll make a fool of yourself.' He took up from the table a volume of the encyclopedia in which, the day before, he had been looking up Pestalozzi, and turned over the pages in search of something to restore his equanimity. An article on perspective proved to be the very thing. Wholly unromantic in character, its copious presentment of hard fact relieved his mind, and he was soon threading his way along paths of knowledge to which he was little accustomed. He applied his remedy with such persistence that when four or five minutes had passed, he felt sufficiently composed to return to the study. He framed, as he went, a suitable form of words with which to open the conversation, and took with him his register of Banns of Marriage, of which he thought he foresaw the need. As he opened the study-door, the book fell from his hands to the ground, so completely was he overcome by surprise, for he found the room empty. The lady had disappeared; her chair stood vacant before him.

Mr Batchel sat down for a moment, and then rang the bell. It was answered by the boy who always attended upon him.

'When did the lady go?' asked Mr Batchel.

The boy looked bewildered.

'The lady you showed into the study before I came.'

'Please, sir, I never shown anyone into the study; I never do when you're out.'

'There was a lady here,' said Mr Batchel, 'when I returned.'

The boy now looked incredulous.

'Did you not let someone out just now?'

'No, sir,' said the boy. 'I put the chain on the front door as soon as you came in.'

This was conclusive. The chain upon the hall door was an ancient and cumbrous thing, and could not be manipulated without considerable effort, and a great deal of noise. Mr Batchel released the boy, and began to think furiously. He was not, as the reader is well aware, without some experience of the supranormal side of nature, and he knew of course that the visit of this enthralling lady had a purpose. He was beginning to know, however, that it had had an effect. He sat before his fire reproducing her image, and soon gave it up in disgust because his imagination refused to do her justice. He could recover the details of her appearance, but could combine them into nothing that would reproduce the impression she had first made upon him.

He was unable now to concentrate his attention upon the examination papers lying on his table. His mind wandered so often to the other topic that he felt himself to be in danger of marking the answers unfairly. He turned away from his work, therefore, and moved to another chair, where he sat down to read. It was the chair in which she herself had sat, and he made no attempt to pretend that he had chosen it on any other account. He had, in fact, made some discoveries about himself during the last half-hour, and he gave himself another surprise when he came to select his book. In the ordinary course of what he had supposed to be his nature, he would certainly have returned to the article on perspective; it was lying open in the next room, and he had read no more than a tenth part of it. But instead of that, his thoughts went back to a volume he had but once opened, and that for no more than two minutes. He had received the book, by way of birthday present, early in the preceding year, from a relative who had bestowed either no consideration at all, or else a great deal of cunning, upon its selection. It was a collection of seventeenth-century lyrics, which Mr Batchel's single glance had sufficed to condemn. Regarding the one lyric he had read as a sort of literary freak, he had banished the book to one of the spare bedrooms, and had never seen it since. And now, after this long interval, the absurd lines which his eye had but once lighted upon, were recurring to his mind:

> Fair, sweet, and young a prize
> Reserved for your victorious eyes;

and so far from thinking them absurd, as he now recalled them, he went upstairs to fetch the book, in which he was soon absorbed. The lyrics no longer seemed unreasonable. He felt conscious, as he read one after another, of a side of nature that he had strangely neglected, and was obliged to admit that the men whose feelings were set forth in the various sonnets and poems had a fine gift of expression.

> Thus, whilst I look for her in vain,
> Methinks I am a child again,
>   And of my shadow am a-chasing.
> For all her graces are to me
> Like apparitions that I see,
>   But never can come near th'embracing.

No! these men were not, as he had formerly supposed, writing with air, and he felt ashamed at having used the term 'freak' at their expense.

Mr Batchel read more of the lyrics, some of them twice, and one of them much oftener. That one he began to commit to memory, and since the household had retired to rest, to recite aloud. He had been unaware that literature contained anything so beautiful, and as he looked again at the book to recover an expression his memory had lost, a tear fell upon the page. It was a thing so extraordinary that Mr Batchel first looked at the ceiling, but when he found that it was indeed a tear from his own eye he was immoderately pleased with himself. Had not she also shed a tear as she sat upon the same chair? The fact seemed to draw them together.

Contemplation of this sort was, however, a luxury to be enjoyed in something like moderation. Mr Batchel soon laid down his lyric and savagely began to add up columns of marks, by way of discipline; and when he had totalled several pages of these, respect for his normal self had returned with sufficient force to take him off to bed.

The matter of his dreams, or whether he dreamed at all, has not been disclosed. He awoke, at any rate, in a calmer state of mind, and such romantic thoughts as remained were effectually dispelled by the sight of his own countenance when he began to shave. 'Fancy you spouting lyrics,' he said, as he dabbed the brush upon his mouth, and by the time he was ready for breakfast he pronounced himself cured.

The prosaic labours awaiting him in the study were soon forced upon his notice, and for once he did not regret it. Amongst the letters lying upon the breakfast table was one from the secretary who controlled the system of examination. The form of the envelope was too familiar to leave him in doubt as to what it contained. It was a letter which, to a careful man like Mr Batchel, seemed to have the nature of a reproof, inasmuch as it probably asked for information which it had already been his duty to furnish. The contents of the envelope, when he had impatiently torn it open, answered to his expectation—he was formally requested to supply the name and the marks of candidate No 1004, and he wondered, as he ate his breakfast, how he had omitted to return them. He hunted out the paper of No 1004 as soon as the meal was over. The candidate proved to be one Lubrietta Rodria, of whom, of course, he had never heard, and her answers had all been marked. He could not understand why they should have been made the subject of enquiry.

He took her papers in his hand, and looked at them again as he stood with his back to the fire, having lit the pipe which invariably followed his breakfast, and then he discovered something much harder to understand. The marks were not his own. In place of the usual sketchy numerals, hardly decipherable to any but himself, he saw figures which were carefully formed; and the marks assigned to the first answer, as he saw it on the uppermost sheet, were higher than the maximum number obtainable for that question.

Mr Batchel laid down his pipe and seated himself at the table. He was greatly puzzled. As he turned over the sheets of No 1004 he found all the other questions marked in like manner, and making a total of half as much again as the highest possible number. 'Who the dickens,' he said, using a meaningless, but not uncommon expression, 'has been playing with this; and how came I to pass it over?' The need of the moment, however, was to furnish the proper marks to the secretary at Cambridge, and Mr Batchel proceeded to read No 1004 right through.

He soon found that he had read it all before, and the matter began to bristle with queries. It proved, in fact, to be a paper over which he had spent some time, and for a singularly interesting reason. He had learned from a friend in the Indian Civil Service that an exaggerated value was often placed by ambitious Indians and Cingalese upon a European education, and that many aspiring young men declined to take a wife who had not passed this very examination. It was to Mr Batchel a disquieting reflection that his blue pencil was not only marking mistakes, but might at the same time be cancelling matrimonial engagements, and his friend's communication had made him scrupulously careful in examining the work of young ladies in oriental schools. The matter had occurred to him at once as he had examined the answers of Lubrietta Rodria. He perfectly remembered the question upon which her success depended. A problem in logic had been answered by a rambling and worthless argument, to which, somehow, the right conclusion was appended: the conclusion might be a happy guess, or it might have been secured by less honest means, but Mr Batchel, following his usual practice, gave no marks for it. It was not here that he found any cause for hesitation, but when he came to the end of the paper and found that the candidate had only just failed, he had turned back to the critical question, imagined an eligible bachelor awaiting the result of the examination, and then, after a period of vacillation, had hastily put the symbol of failure upon the paper lest he should be tempted to bring his own charity to the rescue of the candidate's logic, and unfairly add the three marks which would suffice to pass her.

As he now read the answer for the second time, the same pitiful thought troubled him, and this time more than before; for over the edge of the paper of No 1004 there persistently arose the image of the young lady with the sapphire ring. It directed the current of his thoughts. Suppose that Lubrietta Rodria were anything like that! and what if the arguments of No 1004 were worthless! Young ladies were notoriously weak in argument, and as strong in conclusions! and after all, the conclusion was correct, and ought not a correct conclusion to have its marks? There followed much more to the same purpose, and in the end Mr Batchel stultified himself by adding the necessary three marks, and passing the candidate.

'This comes precious near to being a job,' he remarked, as he entered the marks upon the form and sealed it in the envelope, 'but No 1004 must pass, this time.' He enclosed in the envelope a request to know why the marks had been asked for, since they had certainly been returned in their proper place. A brief official reply informed him next day that the marks he had returned exceeded the maximum, and must, therefore, have been wrongly entered.

'This,' said Mr Batchel, 'is a curious coincidence.'

Curious as it certainly was, it was less curious than what immediately followed. It was Mr Batchel's practice to avoid any delay in returning these official papers, and he went out, there and then, to post his envelope. The Post Office was no more than a hundred yards from his door, and in three minutes he was in his study again. The first object that met his eye there was a beautiful sapphire ring lying upon the papers of No 1004, which had remained upon the table.

Mr Batchel at once recognized the ring. 'I knew it was precious near a job,' he said, 'but I didn't know that it was as near as this.'

He took up the ring and examined it. It looked like a ring of great value; the stone was large and brilliant, and the setting was of fine workmanship. 'Now what on earth,' said Mr Batchel, 'am I to do with this?'

The nearest jeweller to Stoneground was a competent and experienced tradesman of the old school. He was a member of the local Natural History Society, and in that capacity Mr Batchel had made intimate acquaintance with him. To his jeweller, therefore, he carried the ring, and asked him what he thought of it.

'I'll give you forty pounds for it,' said the jeweller.

Mr Batchel replied that the ring was not his. 'What about the make of it?' he asked. 'Is it English?'

The jeweller replied that it was unmistakably Indian.

'You are sure?' said Mr Batchel.

'Certain,' said the jeweller. 'Major Ackroyd brought home one like it, all but the stone, from Puna; I repaired it for him last year.'

The information was enough, if not more than enough, for

Mr Batchel. He begged a suitable case from his friend the jeweller, and within an hour had posted the ring to Miss Lubrietta Rodria at the European College in Puna. At the same time he wrote to the Principal the letter whose answer is embodied in the preface to this narrative.

Having done this, Mr Batchel felt more at ease. He had given Lubrietta Rodria what he amiably called the benefit of the doubt, but it should never be said that he had been bribed.

The rest of his papers he marked with fierce justice. A great deal of the work, in his zeal, he did twice over, but his conscience amply requited him for the superfluous labour. The last paper was marked within a day of the allotted time, Mr Batchel shortly afterwards received his cheque, and was glad to think that the whole matter was at an end.

That Lubrietta had been absent from India whilst her relatives and attendants were trying to restore her to consciousness, he had good reason to know. His friends, for the most part, took a very narrow view of human nature and its possibilities, so that he kept his experience, for a long time, to himself; there were personal reasons for not discussing the incident. The reader has been already told upon what understanding it is recorded here.

There remains, however, an episode which Mr Batchel all but managed to suppress. Upon the one occasion when he allowed himself to speak of this matter, he was being pressed for a description of the sapphire ring, and was not very successful in his attempt to describe it. There was no reason, of course, why this should lay his good faith under suspicion. Few of us could pass an examination upon objects with which we are supposed to be familiar, or say which of our tables have three legs, and which four.

One of Mr Batchel's auditors, however, took a captious view of the matter, and brusquely remarked, in imitation of a more famous sceptic, 'I don't believe there's no sich a thing.'

Mr Batchel, of course, recognized the phrase, and it was his eagerness to establish his credit that committed him at this point to a last disclosure about Lubrietta. He drew a sapphire ring from his pocket, handed it to the incredulous auditor, and addressed him in the manner of Mrs Gamp.

'What! you bage creetur, have I had this ring three year or more to be told there ain't no such a thing. Go along with you.'

'But I thought the ring was sent back,' said more than one.

'How did you come by it?' said all the others.

Mr Batchel thereupon admitted that he had closed his story prematurely. About six weeks after the return of the ring to Puna he had found it once again upon his table, returned through the post. Enclosed in the package was a note which Mr Batchel, being now committed to this part of the story, also passed round for inspection. It ran as follows:

Accept the ring, dear one, and wear it for my sake. Fail not to think sometimes of her whom you have made happy—L R.

'What on earth am I to do with this?' Mr Batchel had asked himself again. And this time he had answered the question, after the briefest possible delay, by slipping the ring upon his fourth finger.

The book of Lyrics remained downstairs amongst the books in constant use. Mr Batchel can repeat at least half of the collection from memory.

He knows well enough that such terms as 'dear one' are addressed to bald gentlemen only in a Pickwickian sense, but even with that sense the letter gives him pleasure.

He admits that he thinks very often of 'her whom he has made happy', but that he cannot exclude from his thoughts at these times an ungenerous regret. It is that he has also made happy a nameless oriental gentleman whom he presumptuously calls 'the other fellow'.

THE ROCKERY

THE vicar's garden at Stoneground has certainly been enclosed for more than seven centuries, and during the whole of that time its almost sacred privacy has been regarded as permanent and unchangeable. It has remained for the innovators of later and more audacious days to hint that it might be given into other hands, and still carry with it no curse that should make a new possessor hasten to undo his irreverence. Whether there can be warrant for such confidence, time will show. The experiences already related will show that the privacy of the garden has been counted upon both by good men and worse. And here is a story, in its way, more strange than any.

By way of beginning, it may be well to describe a part of the garden not hitherto brought into notice. That part lies on the western boundary, where the garden slopes down to a sluggish stream, hardly a stream at all, locally known as the Lode. The Lode bounds the garden on the west along its whole length, and there the moor-hen builds her nest, and the kingfisher is sometimes, but in these days too rarely, seen. But the centre of vision, as it were, of this western edge lies in a cluster of tall elms. Towards these all the garden paths converge, and about their base is raised a bank of earth, upon which is heaped a rockery of large stones lately overgrown with ferns.

Mr Batchel's somewhat prim taste in gardening had long

resented this disorderly bank. In more than one place in his garden had wild confusion given place to a park-like trimness, and there were not a few who would say that the change was not for the better. Mr Batchel, however, went his own way, and in due time determined to remove the rockery. He was puzzled by its presence; he could see no reason why a bank should have been raised about the feet of the elms, and surmounted with stones; not a ray of sunshine ever found its way there, and none but coarse and uninteresting plants had established themselves. Whoever had raised the bank had done it ignorantly, or with some purpose not easy for Mr Batchel to conjecture.

Upon a certain day, therefore, in the early part of December, when the garden had been made comfortable for its winter rest, he began, with the assistance of his gardener, to remove the stones into another place.

We do but speak according to custom in this matter, and there are few readers who will not suspect the truth, which is that the gardener began to remove the stones, whilst Mr Batchel stood by and delivered criticisms of very slight value. Such strength, in fact, as Mr Batchel possessed had concentrated itself upon the mind, and somewhat neglected his body, and what he called help, during his presence in the garden, was called by another name when the gardener and his boy were left to themselves, with full freedom of speech.

There were few of the stones rolled down by the gardener that Mr Batchel could even have moved, but his astonishment at their size soon gave place to excitement at their appearance. His antiquarian tastes were strong, and were soon busily engaged. For, as the stones rolled down, his eyes were feasted, in a rapid succession, by capitals of columns, fragments of moulded arches and mullions, and other relics of ecclesiastical building.

Repeatedly did he call the gardener down from his work to put these fragments together, and before long there were several complete lengths of arcading laid upon the path. Stones which, perhaps, had been separated for centuries, once more came together, and Mr Batchel, rubbing his hands in excited satisfaction, declared that he might recover the best parts of a church by the time the rockery had been demolished.

The interest of the gardener in such matters was of a milder kind. 'We must go careful,' he merely observed, 'when we come to the organ.' They went on removing more and more stones, until at length the whole bank was laid bare, and Mr Batchel's chief purpose achieved. How the stones were carefully arranged, and set up in other parts of the garden, is well known, and need not concern us now.

One detail, however, must not be omitted. A large and stout stake of yew, evidently of considerable age, but nevertheless quite sound, stood exposed after the clearing of the bank. There was no obvious reason for its presence, but it had been well driven in, so well that the strength of the gardener, or, if it made any difference, of the gardener and Mr Batchel together, failed even to shake it. It was not unsightly, and might have remained where it was, had not the gardener exclaimed, 'This is the very thing we want for the pump.' It was so obviously 'the very thing' that its removal was then and there decided upon.

The pump referred to was a small iron pump used to draw water from the Lode. It had been affixed to many posts in turn, and defied them all to hold it. Not that the pump was at fault. It was a trifling affair enough. But the pumpers were usually garden-boys, whose impatient energy had never failed, before many days, to wriggle the pump away from its supports. When the gardener had, upon one occasion, spent half a day in attaching it firmly to a post, they had at once shaken out the post itself. Since, therefore, the matter was causing daily inconvenience, and the gardener becoming daily more concerned for his reputation as a rough carpenter, it was natural for him to exclaim, 'This is the very thing.' It was a better stake than he had ever used, and as had just been made evident, a stake that the ground would hold.

'Yes!' said Mr Batchel, 'it is the very thing; but can we get it up?' The gardener always accepted this kind of query as a challenge, and replied only by taking up a pick and setting to work, Mr Batchel, as usual, looking on, and making, every now and then, a fruitless suggestion. After a few minutes, however, he made somewhat more than a suggestion. He darted forward and laid his hand upon the pick. 'Don't you see some copper?' he asked quickly.

Every man who digs knows what a hiding place there is in the earth. The monotony of spade work is always relieved by a hope of turning up something unexpected. Treasure lies dimly behind all these hopes, so that the gardener, having seen Mr Batchel excited over so much that was precious from his own point of view, was quite ready to look for something of value to an ordinary reasonable man. Copper might lead to silver, and that, in turn, to gold. At Mr Batchel's eager question, therefore, he peered into the hole he had made, and examined everything there that might suggest the rounded form of a coin.

He soon saw what had arrested Mr Batchel. There was a lustrous scratch on the side of the stake, evidently made by the pick, and though the metal was copper, plainly enough, the gardener felt that he had been deceived, and would have gone on with his work. Copper of that sort gave him no sort of excitement, and only a feeble interest.

Mr Batchel, however, was on his hands and knees. There was a small irregular plate of copper nailed to the stake; without any difficulty he tore it away from the nails, and soon scraped it clean with a shaving of wood; then, rising to his feet, he examined his find.

There was an inscription upon it, so legible as to need no deciphering. It had been roughly and effectually made with a hammer and nail, the letters being formed by series of holes punched deeply into the metal, and what he read was:

MOVE NOT THIS
STAKE, NOV 1, 1702

But to move the stake was what Mr Batchel had determined upon, and the metal plate he held in his hand interested him chiefly as showing how long the post had been there. He had happened, as he supposed, upon an ancient landmark. The discovery, recorded elsewhere, of a well, near to the edge of his present lawn, had shown him that his premises had once been differently arranged. One of the minor antiquarian tasks he had set himself was to discover and record the old arrangement, and he felt that the position of this stake would help him. He felt no doubt of its being a point upon the western limit of the garden; not improbably marked in this way to show where the garden began, and where ended the ancient hauling-way, which had been secured to the public for purposes of navigation.

The gardener, meanwhile, was proceeding with his work. With no small difficulty he removed the rubble and clay which accounted for the firmness of the stake. It grew dark as the work went on, and a distant clock struck five before it was completed. Five was the hour at which the gardener usually went home; his day began early. He was not, however, a man to leave a small job unfinished, and he went on loosening the earth with his pick, and trying the effect, at intervals, upon the firmness of the stake. It naturally began to give, and could be moved from side to side through a space of some few inches. He lifted out the loosened stones, and loosened more. His pick struck iron, which, after loosening, proved to be links of a rusted chain. 'They've buried a lot of rubbish in this hole,' he remarked, as he went on loosening the chain, which, in the growing darkness, could hardly be seen. Mr Batchel, meanwhile, occupied himself in a simpler task of working the stake to and fro, by way of loosening its hold. Ultimately it began to move with greater freedom. The gardener laid down his tool and grasped the stake, which his master was still holding; their combined efforts succeeded at once; the stake was lifted out.

It turned out to be furnished with an unusually long and sharp point, which explained the firmness of its hold upon the ground. The gardener carried it to the neighbourhood of the pump, in readiness for its next purpose, and made ready to go home. He would drive the stake tomorrow, he said, in the new place, and make the pump so secure that not even the boys could shake it. He also spoke of some designs he had upon the chain, should it prove to be of any considerable length. He was an ingenious man, and his skill in converting discarded articles to new uses was embarrassing to his master. Mr Batchel, as has been said, was a prim gardener, and he had no liking for makeshift devices. He had that day seen his runner beans trained upon a length of old gas-piping, and had no intention of leaving the gardener in possession of such a treasure as a rusty chain. What he said, however, and said with truth, was that he wanted the chain for himself. He had no practical use for it, and hardly expected it to yield him any interest. But a chain buried in 1702 must be examined—nothing ancient comes amiss to a man of antiquarian tastes.

Mr Batchel had noticed, whilst the gardener had been carrying away the stake, that the chain lay very loosely in the earth. The pick had worked well round it. He said, therefore, that the chain must be lifted out and brought to him upon the morrow, bade his gardener goodnight, and went in to his fireside.

This will appear to the reader to be a record of the merest trifles, but all readers will accept the reminder that there is no such thing as a trifle, and that what appears to be trivial has that appearance only so long as it stands alone. Regarded in the light of their consequences, those matters which have seemed to be least in importance, turn out, often enough, to be the greatest. And these trifling occupations, as we may call them for the last time, of Mr Batchel and the gardener, had consequences which shall now be set down as Mr Batchel himself narrated them. But we must take events in their order. At present Mr Batchel is at his fireside, and his gardener at home with his family. The stake is removed, and the hole, in which lies some sort of an iron chain, is exposed.

Upon this particular evening Mr Batchel was dining out. He was a good-natured man, with certain mild powers of entertainment, and his presence as an occasional guest was not unacceptable at some of the more considerable houses of the neighbourhood. And let us hasten to observe that he was not a guest who made any great impression upon the larders or the cellars of his hosts. He liked port, but he liked it only of good quality, and in small quantity. When he returned from a dinner party, therefore, he was never either in a surfeited condition of body, or in any confusion of mind. Not uncommonly after his return upon such occasions did he perform accurate work. Unfinished contributions to sundry local journals were seldom absent from his desk. They were his means of recreation. There they awaited convenient intervals of leisure, and Mr Batchel was accustomed to say that of these intervals he found none so productive as a late hour, or hour and a half, after a dinner party.

Upon the evening in question he returned, about an hour before midnight, from dining at the house of a retired officer residing in the neighbourhood, and the evening had been somewhat less enjoyable than usual. He had taken in to dinner a young lady who had too persistently assailed him with antiquarian questions. Now Mr Batchel did not like talking what he regarded as 'shop', and was not much at home with young ladies, to whom he knew that, in the nature of things, he could be but imperfectly acceptable. With infinite good will towards them, and a genuine liking for their presence, he felt that he had but little to offer them in exchange. There was so little in common between his life and theirs. He felt distinctly at his worst when he found himself treated as a mere scrap-book of information. It made him seem, as he would express it, de-humanized.

Upon this particular evening the young lady allotted to him, perhaps at her own request, had made a scrap-book of him, and he had returned home somewhat discontented, if also somewhat amused. His discontent arose from having been deprived of the general conversation he so greatly, but so rarely, enjoyed. His amusement was caused by the incongruity between a very light-hearted young lady and the subject upon which she had made him talk, for she had talked of nothing else but modes of burial.

He began to recall the conversation as he lit his pipe and dropped into his armchair. She had either been reflecting deeply upon the matter, or, as seemed to Mr Batchel, more probable, had read something and half forgotten it. He recalled her questions, and the answers by which he had vainly tried to lead her to a more attractive topic. For example:

She: 'Will you tell me why people were buried at crossroads?'

He: 'Well, consecrated ground was so jealously guarded that a criminal would be held to have forfeited the right to be buried amongst Christian folk. His friends would therefore choose cross-roads where there was set a wayside cross, and make his grave at the foot of it. In some of my journeys in Scotland I have seen crosses.'

But the young lady had refused to be led into Scotland. She had stuck to her subject.

She: 'Why have coffins come back into use? There is nothing in our Burial Service about a coffin.'

He: 'True, and the use of the coffin is due, in part, to an ignorant notion of confining the corpse, lest, like Hamlet's father, he should walk the earth. You will have noticed that the corpse is always carried out of the house feet foremost, to suggest a final exit, and that the grave is often covered with a heavy slab. Very curious epitaphs are to be found on these slabs.'

But she was not to be drawn into the subject of epitaphs. She had made him tell of other devices for confining spirits to their prison, and securing the peace of the living, especially of those adopted in the case of violent and mischievous men. Altogether an unusual sort of young lady.

The conversation, however, had revived his memories of what was, after all, a matter of some interest, and he determined to look through his parish registers for records of exceptional burials. He was surprised at himself for never having done it. He dismissed the matter from his mind for the time being, and as it was a bright moonlight night he thought he would finish his pipe in the garden.

Therefore, although midnight was close at hand, he strolled complacently round his garden, enjoying the light of the moon no less than in the daytime he would have enjoyed the sun; and thus it was that he arrived at the scene of his labours upon the old rockery. There was more light than there had been at the end of the afternoon, and when he had walked up the bank, and stood over the hole we have already described, he could distinctly see the few exposed links of the iron chain. Should he remove it at once to a place of safety, out of the way of the gardener? It was about time for bed. The city clocks were then striking midnight. He would let the chain decide. If it came out easily he would remove it; otherwise, it should remain until morning.

The chain came out more than easily. It seemed to have a force within itself. He gave but a slight tug at the free end with a view of ascertaining what resistance he had to encounter, and immediately found himself lying upon his back with the chain in his hand. His back had fortunately turned towards an elm three feet away which broke his fall, but there had been violence enough to cause him no little surprise.

The effort he had made was so slight that he could not account for having lost his feet; and being a careful man, he was a little anxious about his evening coat, which he was still wearing. The chain, however, was in his hand, and he made haste to coil it into a portable shape, and to return to the house.

Some fifty yards from the spot was the northern boundary of the garden, a long wall with a narrow lane beyond. It was not unusual, even at this hour of the night, to hear footsteps there. The lane was used by railway men, who passed to and from their work at all hours, as also by some who returned late from entertainments in the neighbouring city.

But Mr Batchel, as he turned back to the house, with his chain over one arm, heard more than footsteps. He heard for a few moments the unmistakable sound of a scuffle, and then a piercing cry, loud and sharp, and a noise of running. It was such a cry as could only have come from one in urgent need of help.

Mr Batchel dropped his chain. The garden wall was some ten feet high and he had no means of scaling it. But he ran quickly into the house, passed out by the hall door into the street, and so towards the lane without a moment's loss of time.

Before he has gone many yards he sees a man running from the lane with his clothing in great disorder, and this man, at the sight of Mr Batchel, darts across the road, runs along in the shadow of an opposite wall and attempts to escape.

The man is known well enough to Mr Batchel. It is one Stephen Medd, a respectable and sensible man, by occupation a shunter, and Mr Batchel at once calls out to ask what has happened. Stephen, however, makes no reply but continues to run along the shadow of the wall, whereupon Mr Batchel crosses over and intercepts him, and again asks what is amiss. Stephen answers wildly and breathlessly, 'I'm not going to stop here, let me go home.'

As Mr Batchel lays his hand upon the man's arm and draws him into the light of the moon, it is seen that his face is streaming with blood from a wound near the eye.

He is somewhat calmed by the familiar voice of Mr Batchel, and is about to speak, when another scream is heard from the lane. The voice is that of a boy or woman, and no sooner does Stephen hear it than he frees himself violently from Mr Batchel and makes away towards his home. With no less speed does Mr Batchel make for the lane, and finds about half way down a boy lying on the ground wounded and terrified.

At first the boy clings to the ground, but her, too, is soon reassured by Mr Batchel's voice, and allows himself to be lifted on to his feet. His wound is also in the face, and Mr Batchel takes the boy into his house, bathes and plasters his wound, and soon restores him to something like calm. He is what is termed a call-boy, employed by the Railway Company to awaken drivers at all hours, and give them their instructions.

Mr Batchel is naturally impatient for the moment he can question the boy about his assailant, who is presumably also the assailant of Stephen Medd. No one had been visible in the lane, though the moon shone upon it from end to end. At the first available moment, therefore, he asks the boy, 'Who did this?'

The answer came, without any hesitation, 'Nobody'. 'There was nobody there,' he said, 'and all of a sudden somebody hit me with an iron thing.'

Then Mr Batchel asked, 'Did you see Stephen Medd?' He was becoming greatly puzzled.

The boy replied that he had seen Mr Medd 'a good bit in front,' with nobody near him, and that all of a sudden someone knocked him down.

Further questioning seemed useless. Mr Batchel saw the boy to his home, left him at the door, and returned to bed, but not to sleep. He could not cease from thinking, and he could think of nothing but assaults from invisible hands. Morning seemed long in coming, but came at last.

Mr Batchel was up betimes and made a very poor breakfast. Dallying with the morning paper, rather than reading it, his eye was arrested by a headline about 'Mysterious assaults in Elmham.' He felt that he had mysteries of his own to occupy him and was in no mood to be interested in more assaults. But he had some knowledge of Elmham, a small town ten miles distant from Stoneground, and he read the brief paragraph, which contained no more than the substance of a telegram. It said, however, that three persons had been victims of unaccountable assaults. Two of them had escaped with slight injuries, but the third, a young woman, was dangerously wounded, though still alive and conscious. She declared that she was quite alone in her house and had been suddenly struck with great violence by what felt like a piece of iron, and that she must have bled to death but for a neighbour who heard her cries. The neighbour had at once looked out and seen nobody, but had bravely gone to her friend's assistance.

Mr Batchel laid down his newspaper considerably impressed, as was natural, by the resemblance of these tragedies to what he had witnessed himself. He was in no condition, after his excitement and his sleepless night, to do his usual work. His mind reverted to the conversation at the dinner party and the trifle of antiquarian research it had suggested. Such occupation had often served him when he found himself suffering from a cold, or otherwise indisposed for more serious work. He would get the registers and collect what entries there might be of irregular burial.

He found only one such entry, but that one was enough. There was a note dated All Hallows, 1702, to this effect:

> This day did a vagrant from Elmham beat cruelly to death two poor men who had refused him alms, and upon a hue and cry being raised, took his own life. He was buried in one Parson's Close with a stake through his body and his arms confined in chains, and stoutly covered in.

No further news came from Elmham. Either the effort had been exhausted, or its purpose achieved. But what could have led the young lady, a stranger to Mr Batchel and to his garden, to hit upon so appropriate a topic? Mr Batchel could not answer the question as he put it to himself again and again during the day.

He only knew that she had given him a warning, by which, to his shame and regret, he had been too obtuse to profit.

THE INDIAN LAMPSHADE

WHAT has been already said of Mr Batchel will have sufficed to inform the reader that he is a man of very settled habits. The conveniences of life, which have multiplied so fast of late, have never attracted him, even when he has heard of them. Inconveniences to which he is accustomed have always seemed to him preferable to conveniences with which he is unfamiliar. To this day, therefore, he writes with a quill, winds up his watch with a key, and will drink no soda-water but from a tumbling bottle with the cork wired to its neck.

The reader accordingly will learn without surprise that Mr Batchel continues to use the reading-lamp he acquired thirty years ago as a freshman in college. He still carries it from room to room as occasion requires, and ignores all other means of illumination. It is an inexpensive lamp of very poor appearance, and dates from a time when labour-saving was not yet a fine art. It cannot be lighted without the removal of several of its parts, and it is extinguished by the primitive device of blowing down the chimney. What has always shocked the womenfolk of the Batchel family, however, is the lamp's unworthiness of its surroundings. Mr Batchel's house is furnished in dignified and comfortable style, but the handsome lamp, surmounting a fluted brazen column, which his relatives bestowed upon him at his institution, is still unpacked.

One of his younger and subtler relatives succeeded in damaging the old lamp, as she thought, irretrievably, by a well-planned accident, but found it still in use a year later, most atrociously repaired. The whole family, and some outsiders, had conspired to attack the offending lamp, and it had withstood them all.

The single victory achieved over Mr Batchel in this matter is quite recent, and was generally unexpected. A cousin who had gone out to India as a bride, and that of Mr Batchel's making, had sent him an Indian lampshade. The association was pleasing. The shade was decorated with Buddhist figures which excited Mr Batchel's curiosity, and to the surprise of all his friends he set it on the lamp and there allowed it to remain. It was not, however, the figures which had reconciled him to this novel and somewhat incongruous addition to the old lamp. The singular colour of the material had really attracted him. It was a bright orange-red, like no colour he had ever seen, and the remarks of visitors whose experience of such things was greater than his own soon justified him in regarding it as unique. No one had seen the colour elsewhere; and of all the tints which have acquired distinctive names, none of the names could be applied without some further qualification. Mr Batchel himself did not trouble about a name, but was quite certain that it was a colour that he liked; and more than that, a colour which had about it some indescribable fascination. When the lamp had been brought in, and the curtains drawn, he used to regard with singular pleasure the interiors of rooms with whose appearance he was unaccustomed to concern himself. The books in his study, and the old-fashioned solid furniture of his dining room, as reflected in the new light, seemed to assume a more friendly aspect, as if they had previously been rigidly frozen, and had now thawed into life. The lampshade seemed to bestow upon the light some active property, and give to the rooms, as Mr Batchel said, the appearance of being wide-awake.

These optical effects, as he called them, were especially noticeable in the dining room, where the convenience of a large table often induced him to spend the evening. Standing in a favourite attitude, with his elbow on the chimney-piece, Mr Batchel found increasing pleasure in contemplating the interior of the room as he saw it reflected in a large old mirror above the fireplace. The great mahogany sideboard across the room, seemed, as he gazed upon it, to be penetrated by the light, and to acquire a softness of outline, and a sort of vivacity, which operated pleasantly upon its owner's imagination. He found himself playfully regretting, for example, that the mirror had no power of recording and reproducing the scenes enacted before it since the close of the eighteenth century, when it had become one of the fixtures of the house. The ruddy light of the lampshade had always a stimulating effect upon his fancy, and some of the verses which describe his visions before the mirror would delight the reader, but that the author's modesty forbids their reproduction. Had he been less firm in this matter we should have inserted here a poem in which Mr Batchel audaciously ventured into the domain of Physics. He endowed his mirror with the power of retaining indefinitely the light which fell upon it, and of reflecting it only when excited by the appropriate stimulus. The passage beginning

> The mirror, whilst men pass upon their way,
> Treasures their image for a later day,

might be derided by students of optics. Mr Batchel has often read it in after days, with amazement, for, when his idle fancies came to be so gravely substantiated, he found that in writing the verses he had stumbled upon a new fact—a fact based as soundly, as will soon appear, upon experiment, as those which the text books use in arriving at the better-known properties of reflection.

He was seated in his dining room one frosty evening in January. His chair was drawn up to the fire, and the upper part of the space behind him was visible in the mirror. The brighter and clearer light thrown down by the shade was shining upon his book. It is the fate of most of us to receive visits when we should best like to be alone, and Mr Batchel allowed an impatient exclamation to escape him, when, at nine o'clock on this evening, he heard the door-bell. A minute later, the boy announced 'Mr Mutcher,' and Mr Batchel, with such affability as he could hastily assume, rose to receive the caller. Mr Mutcher was the Deputy Provincial Grand Master of the Ancient Order of Gleaners, and the formality of his manner accorded with the gravity of his title. Mr Batchel soon became aware that the rest of the evening was doomed. The Deputy Provincial Grand Master had come to discuss the probable effect of the Insurance Act upon Friendly Societies, of which Mr Batchel was an ardent supporter. He attended their meetings, in some cases kept their accounts, and was always apt to be consulted in their affairs. He seated Mr Mutcher, therefore, in a chair on the opposite side of the fireplace, and gave him his somewhat reluctant attention.

'This,' said Mr Mutcher, as he looked round the room, 'is a cosy nook on a cold night. I cordially appreciate your kindness, Reverend Sir, in affording me this interview, and the comfort of your apartment leads me to wish that it might be more protracted.'

Mr Batchel did his best not to dissent, and as he settled himself for a long half-hour, began to watch the rise and fall, between two lines upon the distant wallpaper of the shadow of Mr Mutcher's side-whisker, as it seemed to beat time to his measured speech.

The D.P.G.M. (for these functionaries are usually designated by initials) was not a man to be hurried into brevity. His style had been studiously acquired at Lodge meetings, and Mr Batchel knew it well enough to be prepared for a lengthy preamble.

'I have presumed,' said Mr Mutcher, as he looked straight before him into the mirror, 'to trespass upon your Reverence's forbearance, because there are one or two points upon this new Insurance Act which seem calculated to damage our long-continued prosperity—I say long-continued prosperity,' repeated Mr Mutcher, as though Mr Batchel had missed the phrase. 'I had the favour of an interview yesterday,' he went on, 'with the Sub-Superintendent of the Perseverance Accident and General (these were household words in circles which Mr Batchel frequented, so that he was at no loss to understand them), and he was unanimous with me in agreeing that the matter called for careful consideration. There are one or two of our rules which we know to be essential to the welfare of our Order, and yet which will have to go by the board—I say by the board—as from July next. Now we are not Medes, nor yet Persians'—Mr Mutcher was about to repeat 'Persians' when he was observed to look hastily round the room and then to turn deadly pale. Mr Batchel rose and hastened to his support; he was obviously unwell. The visitor, however, made a strong effort, rose from his chair at once, saying 'Pray allow me to take leave,' and hurried to the door even as he said the words. Mr Batchel, with real concern, followed him with the offer of brandy, or whatever might afford relief. Mr Mutcher did not so much as pause to reply. Before Mr Batchel could reach him he had crossed the hall, and the door-knob was in his hand. He thereupon opened the door and passed into the street without another word. More unaccountably still, he went away at a run, such as ill became his somewhat majestic figure, and Mr Batchel closed the door and returned to the dining-room in a state of bewilderment. He took up his book, and sat down again in his chair. He did not immediately begin to read, but set himself to review Mr Mutcher's unaccountable behaviour, and as he raised his eyes to the mirror he saw an elderly man standing at the sideboard.

Mr Batchel quickly turned round, and as he did so, recalled the similar movement of his late visitor. The room was empty. He turned again to the mirror, and the man was still there—

evidently a servant—one would say without much hesitation, the butler. The cut-away coat, and white stock, the clean-shaven chin, and close-trimmed side-whiskers, the deftness and decorum of his movements were all characteristic of a respectable family servant, and he stood at the sideboard like a man who was at home there.

Another object, just visible above the frame of the mirror, caused Mr Batchel to look round again, and again to see nothing unusual. But what he saw in the mirror was a square oaken box some few inches deep, which the butler was proceeding to unlock. And at this point Mr Batchel had the presence of mind to make an experiment of extraordinary value. He removed, for a moment, the Indian shade from the lamp, and laid it upon the table, and thereupon the mirror showed nothing but empty space and the frigid lines of the furniture. The butler had disappeared, as also had the box, to reappear the moment the shade was restored to its place.

As soon as the box was opened, the butler produced a bundled handkerchief which his left hand had been concealing under the tails of his coat. With his right hand he removed the contents of the handkerchief, hurriedly placed them in the box, closed the lid, and having done this, left the room at once. His later movements had been those of a man in fear of being disturbed. He did not even wait to lock the box. He seemed to have heard someone coming.

Mr Batchel's interest in the box will subsequently be explained. As soon as the butler had left, he stood before the mirror and examined it carefully. More than once, as he felt the desire for a closer scrutiny, he turned to the sideboard itself, where of course no box was to be seen, and returned to the mirror unreasonably disappointed. At length, with the image of the box firmly impressed upon his memory, he sat down again in his chair, and reviewed the butler's conduct, or as he doubted he would have to call it, misconduct. Unfortunately for Mr Batchel, the contents of the handkerchief had been indistinguishable. But for the butler's alarm, which caused him to be moving away from the box even whilst he was placing the thing within it, the mirror could not have shown as much as it did. All that had been made evident was that the man had something to conceal, and that it was surreptitiously done.

'Is this all?' said Mr Batchel to himself as he sat looking into the mirror, 'or is it only the end of the first Act?' The question was, in a measure, answered by the presence of the box. That, at all events would have to disappear before the room could resume its ordinary aspect; and whether it was to fade out of sight or to be removed by the butler, Mr Batchel did not intend to be looking another way at the time. He had not seen, although perhaps Mr Mutcher had, whether the butler had brought it in, but he was determined to see whether he took it out.

He had not gazed into the mirror for many minutes before he learned that there was to be a second Act. Quite suddenly, a woman was at the sideboard. She had darted to it, and the time taken in passing over half the length of the mirror had been altogether too brief to show what she was like. She now stood with her face to the sideboard, entirely concealing the box from view, and all Mr Batchel could determine was that she was tall of stature, and that her hair was raven-black, and not in very good order. In his anxiety to see her face, he called aloud, 'Turn round.' Of course, he understood, when he saw that his cry had been absolutely without effect, that it had been a ridiculous thing to do. He turned his head again for a moment to assure himself that the room was empty, and to remind himself that the curtain had fallen, perhaps a century before, upon the drama—he began to think of it as a tragedy—that he was witnessing. The opportunity, however, of seeing the woman's features was not denied him. She turned her face full upon the mirror—this is to speak as if we described the object rather than the image—so that Mr Batchel saw it plainly before him; it was a handsome, cruel-looking face, of waxen paleness, with fine, distended, lustrous eyes. The woman looked hurriedly round the room, looked twice towards the door, and then opened the box.

'Our respectable friend was evidently observed,' said Mr Batchel. 'If he has annexed anything belonging to this magnificent female, he is in for a bad quarter of an hour.' He would have given a great deal, for once, to have had a sideboard backed by a looking glass, and lamented that the taste of the day had been too good to tolerate such a thing. He would have then been able to see what was going on at the oaken box. As it was, the operations were concealed by the figure of the woman. She was evidently busy with her fingers; her elbows, which showed plainly enough, were vibrating with activity. In a few minutes there was a final movement of the elbows simultaneously away from her sides, and it showed, as plainly as if the hands had been visible, that something had been plucked asunder. It was just such a movement as accompanies the removal, after a struggle, of the close-fitting lid of a canister.

'What next?' said Mr Batchel, as he observed the movement, and interpreted it as the end of the operation at the box. 'Is this the end of the second Act?'

He was soon to learn that it was not the end, and that the drama of the mirror was indeed assuming the nature of tragedy. The woman closed the box and looked towards the door, as she had done before; then she made as if she would dart out of the room, and found her movement suddenly arrested. She stopped dead, and, in a moment, fell loosely to the ground. Obviously she had swooned away.

Mr Batchel could then see nothing, except that the box remained in its place on the sideboard, so that he arose and stood close up to the mirror in order to obtain a view of the whole stage, as he called it. It showed him, in the wider view he now obtained, the woman lying in a heap upon the carpet, and a grey-wigged clergyman standing in the doorway of the room.

'The vicar of Stoneground, without a doubt,' said Mr Batchel. 'The household of my reverend predecessor is not doing well by him; to judge from the effect of his appearance upon this female, there's something serious afoot. Poor old man,' he added, as the clergyman walked into the room.

This expression of pity was evoked by the vicar's face. The marks of tears were upon his cheeks, and he looked weary and ill. He stood for a while looking down upon the woman who had swooned away, and then stooped down, and gently opened her hand.

Mr Batchel would have given a great deal to know what the vicar found there. He took something from her, stood erect for a moment with an expression of consternation upon his face; then his chin dropped, his eyes showed that he had lost consciousness, and he fell to the ground, very much as the woman had fallen.

The two lay, side by side, just visible in the space between the table and the sideboard. It was a curious and pathetic situation. As the clergyman was about to fall, Mr Batchel had turned to save him, and felt a real distress of helplessness at being reminded again that it was but an image that he had looked upon. The two persons now lying upon the carpet had been for some hundred years beyond human aid. He could no more help them than he could help the wounded at Waterloo. He was tempted to relieve his distress by removing the shade of the lamp; he had even laid his hand upon it, but the feeling of curiosity was now become too strong, and he knew that he must see the matter to its end.

The woman first began to revive. It was to be expected, as she had been the first to go. Had not Mr Batchel seen her face in the mirror, her first act of consciousness would have astounded him. Now it only revolted him. Before she had sufficiently recovered to raise herself upon her feet, she forced open the lifeless hands beside her and snatched away the contents of that which was not empty; and as she did this, Mr Batchel saw the glitter of precious stones. The woman was soon upon her feet and making feebly for the door, at which she paused to leer at the prostrate figure of the clergyman before she disappeared into the hall. She appeared no more, and Mr Batchel felt glad to be rid of her presence.

The old vicar was long in coming to his senses; as he began to move, there stood in the doorway the welcome figure of the butler. With infinite gentleness he raised his master to his feet, and with a strong arm supported him out of the room, which at last, stood empty.

'That, at least,' said Mr Batchel, 'is the end of the second Act. I doubt whether I could have borne much more. If that awful woman comes back I shall remove the shade and have done with it all. Otherwise, I shall hope to learn what becomes of the box, and whether my respectable friend who has just taken out his master is, or is not, a rascal.' He had been genuinely moved by what he had seen, and was conscious of feeling something like exhaustion. He dare not, however, sit down, lest he should lose anything important of what remained. Neither the door nor the lower part of the room was visible from his chair, so that he remained standing at the chimney-piece, and there awaited the disappearance of the oaken box.

So intently were his eyes fixed upon the box, in which he was especially interested, that he all but missed the next incident. A velvet curtain which he could see through the half closed door had suggested nothing of interest to him. He connected it indefinitely, as it was excusable to do, with the furniture of the house, and only by inadvertence looked at it a second time. When, however, it began to travel slowly along the hall, his curiosity was awakened in a new direction. The butler, helping his master out of the room ten minutes since, had left the door half open, but as the opening was not towards the mirror, only a strip of the hall beyond could be seen. Mr Batchel went to open the door more widely, only to find, of course, that the vividness of the images had again betrayed him. The door of his dining-room was closed, as he had closed it after Mr Mutcher, whose perturbation was now so much easier to understand.

The curtain continued to move across the narrow opening, and explained itself in doing so. It was a pall. The remains it so amply covered were being carried out of the house to their resting-place, and were followed by a long procession of mourners in long cloaks. The hats they held in their black-gloved hands were heavily banded with crepe whose ends descended to the ground, and foremost among them was the old clergyman, refusing the support which two of the chief mourners were in the act of proffering. Mr Batchel, full of sympathy, watched the whole procession pass the door, and not until it was evident that the funeral had left the house did he turn once more to the box. He felt sure that the closing scene of the tragedy was at hand, and it proved to be very near. It was brief and uneventful. The butler very deliberately entered the room, threw aside the window-curtains and drew up the blinds, and then went away at once, taking the box with him. Mr Batchel thereupon blew out his lamp and went to bed, with a purpose of his own to be fulfilled upon the next day.

His purpose may be stated at once. He had recognized the oaken box, and knew that it was still in the house. Three large cupboards in the old library of vicar Whitehead were filled with the papers of a great lawsuit about tithe, dating from the close of the eighteenth century. Amongst these, in the last of the three cupboards, was the box of which so much has been said. It was filled, so far as Mr Batchel remembered, with the assessments for poor's-rate of a large number of landholders concerned in the suit, and these Mr Batchel had never thought it worth his while to disturb. He had gone to rest, however, on this night with the full intention of going carefully through the contents of the box. He scarcely hoped, after so long an interval, to discover any clue to the scenes he had witnessed, but he was determined at least to make the attempt. If he found nothing, he intended that the box should enshrine a faithful record of the transactions in the dining-room.

It was inevitable that a man who had so much of the material of a story should spend a wakeful hour in trying to piece it together. Mr Batchel spent considerably more than an hour in connecting, in this way and that, the butler and his master, the gypsy-looking woman, the funeral, but could arrive at no connexion that satisfied him. Once asleep, he found the problem easier, and dreamed a solution so obvious as to make him wonder that the matter had ever puzzled him. When he awoke in the morning, also, the defects of the solution were so obvious as to make him wonder that he had accepted it; so easily are we satisfied when reason is not there to criticize. But there was still the box, and this Mr Batchel lifted down from the third cupboard, dusted with his towel, and when he was dressed, carried downstairs with him. His breakfast occupied but a small part of a large table, and upon the vacant area he was soon laying, as he examined them, one by one, the documents which the box contained. His recollection of them proved to be right. They were overseers' lists of parochial assessments, of which he soon had a score or more laid upon the table. They were of no interest in themselves, and did nothing to further the matter in hand. They would appear to have been thrust into the box by someone desiring to find a receptacle for them.

In a little while, however, the character of the papers changed. Mr Batchel found himself reading something of another kind, written upon paper of another form and colour.

'Irish bacon to be had of Mr Broadley, hop merchant in Southwark.'

'Raisin wine is kept at the Wine and Brandy vaults in Catherine Street.'

'The best hones at Mr Forsters in Little Britain.'

There followed a recipe for a 'rhumatic mixture', a way of making a polish for mahogany, and other such matters. They were evidently the papers of the butler.

Mr Batchel removed them one by one, as he had removed the others; household accounts followed, one or two private letters, and the advertisement of a lottery, and then he reached a closed compartment at the bottom of the box, occupying about half its area. The lid of the compartment was provided with a bone stud, and Mr Batchel lifted it off and laid it upon the table amongst the papers. He saw at once what the butler had taken from his handkerchief. There was an open pocket-knife, with woeful-looking deposits upon its now rusty blade. There was a delicate human finger, now dry and yellow, and on the finger a gold ring.

Mr Batchel took up this latter pitiful object and removed the ring, even now, not quite easily. He allowed the finger to drop back into the box, which he carried away at once into another room. His appetite for breakfast had left him, and he rang the bell to have the things cleared away, whilst he set himself, with the aid of a lens, to examine the ring.

There had been three large stones, all of which had been violently removed. The claws of their settings were, without exception, either bent outwards, or broken off. Within the ring was engraved, in graceful italic characters, the name *Amey Lee*, and on the broader part, behind the place of the stones

She doth joy double,
And halveth trouble.

This pathetic little love token Mr Batchel continued to hold in his hand as he rehearsed the whole story to which it afforded the clue. He knew that the ring had been set with such stones as there was no mistaking: he remembered only too well how their discovery had affected the aged vicar. But never would he deny himself the satisfaction of hoping that the old man had been spared the distress of learning how the ring had been removed.

The name of Amey Lee was as familiar to Mr Batchel as his own. Twice at least every Sunday during the past seven years had he read it at his feet, as he sat in the chancel, as well as the name of Robert Lee upon an adjacent slab, and he had wondered during the leisurely course of many a meandering hymn whether there was good precedent for the spelling of the name. He made another use now of his knowledge of the pavement. There was a row of tiles along the head of the slabs, and Mr Batchel hastened to fulfil without delay, what he conceived to be his duty. He replaced the ring upon Amey Lee's finger and carried it into the church, and there, having raised one of the tiles with a chisel, gave it decent burial.

Whether the butler ever learned that he had been robbed in his turn, who shall say? His immediate dismissal, after the funeral, seemed inevitable, and his oaken box was evidently placed by him, or by another, where no man heeded it. It still occupies a place amongst the law papers and may lie undisturbed for another century; and when Mr Batchel put it there, without the promised record of events, he returned to the dining room, removed the Indian shade from the lamp, and, having put a lighted match to the edge, watched it slowly burn away.

Only one thing remained. Mr Batchel felt that it would give him some satisfaction to visit Mr Mutcher. His address, as obtained from the District Miscellany of the Order of Gleaners, was 13, Albert Villas, Williamson Street, not a mile away from Stoneground.

Mr Mutcher, fortunately, was at home when Mr Batchel called, and indeed opened the door with a copious apology for being without his coat.

'I hope', said Mr Batchel, 'that you have overcome your indisposition of last Tuesday evening.'

'Don't mention it, your Reverence,' said Mr Mutcher, 'my wife gave me such a talking to when I came 'ome that I was quite ashamed of myself—I say ashamed of myself.'

'She observed that you were unwell,' said Mr Batchel, 'I am sure; but she could hardly blame you for that.'

By this time the visitor had been shown into the parlour, and Mrs Mutcher had appeared to answer for herself.

'I really was ashamed, Sir,' she said, 'to think of the way Mutcher was talking, and a clergyman's 'ouse too. Mutcher is not a man, Sir, that takes anything, not so much as a drop; but he is wonderful partial to cold pork, which never does agree with him, and never did, at night in partic'lar.'

'It was the cold pork, then, that made you unwell?' asked Mr Batchel.

'It was, your Reverence, and it was not,' Mr Mutcher replied, 'for internal discomfort there was none—I say none. But a little light 'eaded it did make me, and I could 'ave swore, your Reverence, saving your presence, that I saw an elderly gentleman carry a box into your room and put it down on the sheffoneer.'

'There was no one there, of course,' observed Mr Batchel.

'No!' replied the D.P.G.M., 'there was not; and the discrepancy was too much for me. I hope you will pardon the abruptness of my departure.'

'Certainly,' said Mr Batchel, 'discrepancies are always embarrassing.'

'And you will allow me one day to resume our discourse upon the subject of National Insurance,' he added, when he showed his visitor to the door.

'I shall not have much leisure,' said Mr Batchel, audaciously, taking all risks, 'until the Greek Kalends.'

'Oh, I don't mind waiting till it does end,' said Mr Mutcher, 'there is no immediate 'urry.'

'It's rather a long time,' remarked Mr Batchel.

'Pray don't mention it,' answered the Deputy Provincial Grand Master, in his best manner. 'But when the time comes, perhaps you'll drop me a line.'

THE PLACE OF SAFETY

'I THANK my governors, teachers, spiritual pastors, and masters,' said Wardle, as he lit a cigar after breakfast, 'that I never acquired a taste for that sort of thing.'

Wardle was a pragmatical and candid friend who paid Mr Batchel occasional visits at Stoneground. He regarded antiquarian tastes as a form of insanity, and it annoyed him to see his host poring over registers, churchwardens' accounts, and documents which he contemptuously alluded to as 'dirty papers.' 'If you would throw those things away, Batchel,' he used to say, 'and read the *Daily Mail*, you'd be a better man for it.'

Mr Batchel replied only with a tolerant smile, and, as his friend went out of doors with his cigar, continued to read the document before him, although it was one he had read twenty times before. It was an inventory of church goods, dated the 6th year of Edward VI—to be exact, 15 May 1552. By a royal order of that year, all church goods, saving only what sufficed for the barest necessities of Divine Service, were collected and deposited in safe hands, there to await further instructions. The instructions, which had not been long delayed, had consisted in a curt order for seizure. Everyone who cares for such matters, knows and laments the grievous spoliation of those times.

Mr Batchel's document, however, proved that the churchwardens of the day were not incapable of self-defence. They were less dumb than sheep before the shearers. For, on the copy of the inventory of which he had become possessed, was written the Commissioners' Report that 'at Stoneground did John Spayn and John Gounthropp, church-wardens, declare upon their othes that two gilded senseres with candellsticks, old paynted clothes, and other implements, were contayned in a chest which was robbed on St Peter's Eve before the first inventorye made.'

Mr Batchel had a shrewd suspicion, which the reader will not improbably share, that John Spayne and his colleague knew more about the robbery than they chose to admit. He said to himself again and again, that the contents of the chest had been carefully concealed until times should mend. But from the point of view of the churchwardens, times had not mended. There was evidence that Stoneground had been in no mood to tolerate censers in the reign of Mary, and it seemed unlikely that any later time could have re-admitted the ancient ritual. On this account, Mr Batchel had never ceased to believe that the contents of the chest lay somewhere near at hand, nor to hope that it might be his lot to discover it.

Whenever there was any work of the nature of excavation or demolition within a hundred yards of the church, Mr Batchel was sure to be there. His presence was very distasteful in most cases, to the workmen engaged, whom it deprived of many intervals of leisure to which they were accustomed when left alone. During a long course of operations connected with the restoration of the church, Mr Batchel's vigilance had been of great advantage to the work, both in raising the standard of industry and in securing attention to details which the builders were quite prepared to overlook. It had, however, brought him no nearer to the censers and other contents of the chest, and when the work was completed, his hopes of discovery had become pitifully slender.

Mr Wardle, notwithstanding his general contempt for antiquarian pursuits, was polite enough to give Mr Batchel's hobbies an occasional place in their conversation, and in this way was informed of the 'stolen' goods. The information, however, gave him no more than a very languid interest.

'Why can't you let the things alone?' he said, 'what's the use of them?'

Mr Batchel felt it all but impossible to answer a man who could say this; yet he made the attempt.

'The historic interest,' he said seriously, 'of censers that were used down to the days of Edward VI is in itself sufficient to justify——'

'Etcetera,' said his friend, interrupting the sentence which even Mr Batchel was not sure of finishing to his satisfaction, 'but it takes so little to justify you antiquarians, with your axes and hammers. What can you do with it when you get it, if you ever do get it?'

'There are two censers,' Mr Batchel mildly observed in correction, 'and other things.'

'All right,' said Wardle; 'tell me about one of them, and leave me to do the multiplication.'

With this permission, Mr Batchel entered upon a general description of such ancient thuribles as he knew of, and Wardle heard him with growing impatience.

'It seems to me,' he burst in at length, 'that what you are making all this pother about is a sort of silver cruet-stand, which was thin metal to begin with, and cleaned down to the thickness of egg-shell before the Commissioners heard of it. At this moment, if it exists, it is a handful of black scrap. If you found it, I wouldn't give a shilling for it; and if I would, it isn't yours to sell. Why can't you let the things alone?'

'But the interest of it,' said Mr Batchel, 'is what attracts me.'

'It's a pity you can't take an interest in something less uninteresting,' said Wardle, petulantly; 'but let me tell you what I think about your censers and all the rest of it. Your churchwardens lied about them, but that's all right; I'd have done the same myself. If their things couldn't be used, they were not going to have them abused, so they put them safely out of the way, your's and everybody's else.'

'I was not proposing to abuse them,' interrupted Mr Batchel.

'Were you proposing to use them?' rejoined Wardle. 'It's one thing or the other, to my mind. There are people who dig out bishops and steal their rings to put in glass cases, but I don't know how they square the police; and it's the same sort of thing you seem to be up to. Let the things alone. You're a Prayer Book man, and just the sort the churchwardens couldn't stomach. You talk fast enough at the Dissenters because they want to collar your property now. Why can't you do as you would be done by?'

Mr Batchel thought it useless to say any more to a man in so unsympathetic an attitude, or to enter upon any defence of the antiquarian researches to which his friend had so crudely referred. He did not much like, however, to be anticipated in a theory of the 'robbery' which he felt to be reasonable and probable. He had hoped to propound the same theory himself, and to receive a suitable compliment upon his penetration. He began, therefore, somewhat irritably, to make the most of conjectures which, at various times, had occurred to him. 'Men of that sort,' he said, 'would have disposed of the censers to some one who could go on using them, and in that case they are not here at all.'

'Men of that sort,' answered Wardle, 'are as careful of their skin as men of any other sort, and besides that, your Stoneground men have a very good notion of sticking to what they have got. The things are here, I daresay, if they are anywhere; but they are not yours, and you have no business to meddle with them. If you would spend your time in something else than poking about after other people's things, you'd get better value for it.'

This brief conversation, in which Mr Batchel had scarcely been allowed the part to which he felt entitled, was in one respect satisfactory. It supported his belief that the censers lay somewhere within reach. In other respects, however, the attitude of Wardle was intolerable. He was evidently out of all sympathy with the quest upon which Mr Batchel was set, and, for their different reasons, each was glad to drop the subject.

During the next two or three days, the matter of the censers was not referred to, if only for lack of opportunity. Wardle was a kind of visitor for whom there was always a welcome at Stoneground, and the welcome was in his case no less cordial on account of his brutal frankness of expression, which, on the whole, his host enjoyed. His pungent criticisms of other men were vastly entertaining to Mr Batchel, who was not so unreasonable as to feel aggrieved at an occasional attack upon himself.

A guest of this unceremonious sort makes but small demands upon his host. Mr Wardle used to occupy himself contentedly and unobtrusively in the house or in the garden whilst his host followed his usual avocations. The two men met at meals, and liked each other none the less because they were apart at most other times. A great part of Mr Wardle's day was passed in the company of the gardener, to whose talk his own master was but an indifferent listener. The visitor and the gardener were both lovers of the soil, and taught each other a great deal as they worked side by side. Mr Wardle found that sort of exercise wholesome, and, as the gardener expressed it, 'was not frit to take his coat off.'

The gardening operations at this time of year were such as Mr Wardle liked. The over-crowded shrubberies were being thinned, and a score or so of young shrubs had to be moved into better quarters. Upon a certain morning, when Mr Batchel was occupied in his study, some aucubas were being transplanted into a strip of ground in front of the house, and Wardle had undertaken the task of digging holes to receive them. It was this task that he suddenly interrupted in order to burst in upon his host in what seemed to the latter a repulsive state of dirt and perspiration.

'Talk of discoveries,' he cried, 'come and see what I've found.'

'Not the censers, I suppose,' said Mr Batchel.

'Censers be hanged,' said Wardle, 'come and look.'

Mr Batchel laid down his pen, with a sigh, and followed Wardle to the front of the house. His guest had made three large holes, each about two feet square, and drawing Mr Batchel to the nearest of them, said 'Look there.'

Mr Batchel looked. He saw nothing, and said so.

'Nothing?' exclaimed Wardle with impatience. 'You see the bottom of the hole, I suppose?'

This Mr Batchel admitted.

'Then,' said Wardle, 'kindly look and see whether you cannot see something else.'

'There is apparently a cylindrical object lying across the angle of your excavation,' said Mr Batchel.

'That,' replied his guest, 'is what you are pleased to call nothing. Let me inform you that the cylindrical object is a piece of thick lead pipe, and that the pipe runs along the whole front of your house.'

'Gas-pipe, no doubt,' said Mr Batchel.

'Is there any gas within a mile of this place?' asked Wardle.

Mr Batchel admitted that there was not, and felt that he had made a needlessly foolish suggestion. He felt safer in the amended suggestion that the object was a water-pipe.

An ironical cross-examination by Mr Wardle disposed of the amended suggestion as completely as he had disposed of the other, and his host began to grow restive. 'If this sort of discovery pleases you,' he said testily, 'I will not grudge you your pleasure, but, to quote your own words, why can't you let it alone?'

'Have you any idea,' said Mr Wardle, 'of the value of this length of piping, at the present price of lead?'

Even Mr Wardle could hardly have suspected his host of knowing anything so preposterous as the price of lead, but he felt himself ill-used when Mr Batchel disclaimed any interest in the matter, and returned to his study.

Wardle had a commercial mind, which elsewhere was the means of securing him a very satisfactory income, and on this account, his host, as he resumed his work indoors, excused what he regarded as a needless interruption.

He little suspected that his friend's commercial mind was to do him the great service of putting him in possession of the censers, and then to do him a disservice even greater.

Had any such connexion so much as suggested itself, Mr Batchel would more willingly have answered to the summons which came an hour later, when the gardener appeared at the window of the study, evidently bursting with information. When he had succeeded in attracting his master's attention, and drawn him away from his desk, it was to say that the whole length of pipe had been uncovered, and found to issue from a well on the south side of the house.

The discovery was at least unexpected, and Mr Batchel went out, even if somewhat grudgingly, to look at the place. He came upon the well, close by the window of his dining-room. It had been covered by a stone slab, now partially removed. The narrow trench which Wardle and the gardener had made in order to expose the pipe, extended eastwards to the corner of the house, and thence along the whole length of the front, probably to serve a pump on the north side, where lay the yard and stables. The pipe itself, Mr Wardle's prize, had been withdrawn, and there remained only a rusted chain which passed from some anchorage beneath the soil, over the lip of the well. Mr Batchel inferred that it had carried, and perhaps carried still, the bucket of former times, and stooped down to see whether he could draw it up. He heard, far below, the light splash of the soil disturbed by his hands; but before he could grasp the chain, he felt himself seized by the waist and held back.

The exaggerated attentions of his gardener had often annoyed Mr Batchel. He was not allowed even to climb a short ladder without having to submit to absurd precautions for his safety, and he would have been much better pleased to have more respect paid to his intelligence, and less to his person. In the present instance, the precaution seemed so unnecessary that he turned about angrily to protest, both against the interference with his movements, and the unseemly force used.

It was at this point that he made a disquieting discovery. He was standing quite alone. The gardener and Mr Wardle were both on the north side of the house, dealing with the only thing they cared about—the lead pipe. Mr Batchel made no further attempt to move the chain; he was, in fact, in some bodily fear, and he returned to his study by the way he had come, in a disordered condition of mind.

Half an hour later, when the gong sounded for luncheon, he was slowly making his way into the dining-room, when he encountered his guest running downstairs from his room, in great spirits. 'A trifle over two hundred-weight!' he exclaimed, as he reached the foot of the staircase, and seemed disappointed that Mr Batchel did not immediately shake hands with him upon so fine a result of the morning's work. Mr Batchel, needless to say, was occupied with other recollections.

'I suppose it is unnecessary to ask,' said he to his guest as he proceeded to carve a chicken, 'whether you believe in ghosts?'

'I do not,' said Wardle promptly, 'why should I?'

'Why not?' asked Mr Batchel.

'Because I've had the advantage of a commercial education,' was the reply, 'instead of learning dead languages and soaking my mind in heathen fables.'

Mr Batchel winced at this disrespectful allusion to the university education of which he was justly proud. He wanted an opinion, however, and the conversation had to go on.

'Your commercial education,' he continued, 'allows you, I daresay, to know what is meant by a hypothetical case.'

'Make it one,' said Wardle.

'Assuming a ghost, then, would it be capable of exerting force upon a material body?'

'Whose?' asked Wardle.

'If you insist upon making it a personal matter,' replied Mr Batchel, 'let us say mine.'

'Let me have the particulars.'

In reply to this, Mr Batchel related his experience at the well.

Mr Wardle merely said 'Pass the salt, I need it.'

Undeterred by the scepticism of his friend, Mr Batchel pressed the point, and upon that, Mr Wardle closed the conversation by observing that since, by hypothesis, ghosts could clank chains, and ring bells, he was bound to suppose them capable of doing any silly thing they chose. 'A month in the City, Batchel,' he gravely added, 'would do you a world of good.'

As soon as the meal was over, Mr Wardle went back to his gardening, whilst his host betook himself to occupations more suited to his tranquil habits. The two did not meet again until dinner; and during that meal, and after it, the conversation turned wholly upon politics, Mr Wardle being congenially occupied until bedtime in demonstrating that the politics of his host had been obsolete for three-quarters of a century. His outdoor exercise, followed by an excellent dinner, had disposed him to retire early; he rose from his chair soon after ten. 'There is one thing,' he pleasantly remarked to his host, 'that I am bound to say in favour of a university education; it has given you a fine taste in victuals.' With this compliment, he said 'good-night,' and went up to bed.

Mr Batchel himself, as the reader knows, kept later hours. There were few nights upon which he omitted to take his walk round the garden when the world had grown quiet, even in unfavourable weather. It was far from favourable upon the present occasion; there was but little moon, and a light rain was falling. He determined, however, to take at least one turn round, and calling his terrier Punch from the kitchen, where he lay in his basket, Mr Batchel went out, with the dog at his heel. He carried, as his custom was, a little electric lamp, by whose aid he liked to peep into birds' nests, and make raids upon slugs and other pests.

They had hardly set out upon their walk when Punch began to show signs of uneasiness. Instead of running to and fro, with his nose to the ground, as he ordinarily did, the terrier remained whining in the rear. Shortly, they came upon a hedgehog lying coiled up in the path; it was a find which the dog was wont to regard as a rare piece of luck, and to assail with delirious enjoyment. Now, for some reason, Punch refused to notice it, and, when it was illuminated for his especial benefit, turned his back upon it and looked up, in a dejected attitude, at his master. The behaviour of the dog was altogether unnatural, and Mr Batchel occupied himself, as they passed on, in trying to account for it, with the animal still whining at his heel. They soon reached the head of the little path which descended to the Lode, and there Mr Batchel found a much harder problem awaiting him, for at the other end of the path he distinctly saw the outline of a boat.

There had been no boat on the Lode for twenty years. Just so long ago the drainage of the district had required that the main sewer should cross the stream at a point some hundred yards below the vicar's boundary fence. There, ever since, a great pipe three feet in diameter had obstructed the passage. It lay just level of the water, and effectually closed it to all traffic. Mr Batchel knew that no boat could pass the place, and that none survived in the parts above it. Yet here was a boat drawn up at the edge of his garden. He looked at it intently for a minute or so, and had no difficulty in making out the form of such a boat as was in common use all over the Fen country—a wide flat-bottomed boat, lying low in the water. The 'sprit' used for punting it along lay projecting over the stern. There was no accounting for such a boat being there: Mr Batchel did not understand how it possibly could be there, and for a while was disposed to doubt whether it actually was. The great drain-pipe was so perfect a defence against intrusion of the kind that no boat had ever passed it. The Lode, when its water was low enough to let a boat go under the pipe, was not deep enough to float it, or wide enough to contain it. Upon this occasion the water was high, and the pipe half submerged, forming an insuperable obstacle. Yet there lay, unmistakably, a boat, within ten yards of the place where Mr Batchel stood trying to account for it.

These ten yards, unfortunately, were impassable. The slope down to the water's edge had to be warily trodden even in dry weather. It was steep and treacherous. After rain it afforded no foothold whatever, and to attempt a descent in the darkness would have been to court disaster. After examining the boat again, therefore, by the light of his little lamp, Mr Batchel proceeded upon his walk, leaving the matter to be investigated by daylight.

The events of this memorable night, however, were but beginning. As he turned from the boat his eye was caught by a white streak upon the ground before him, which extended itself into the darkness and disappeared. It was Punch, in veritable panic, making for home, across flower-beds and other places he well knew to be out of bounds. The whistle he had been trained to obey had no effect upon his flight; he made a lightning dash for the house. Mr Batchel could not help regretting that Wardle was not there to see. His friend held the coursing powers of Punch in great contempt, and was wont to criticize the dog in sporting jargon, whose terms lay beyond the limits of Mr Batchel's vocabulary, but whose general drift was as obvious as it was irritating. The present performance, nevertheless, was so exceptional that it soon began to connect itself in Mr Batchel's mind with the unnatural conduct to which we have already alluded. It was somehow proving to be an uncomfortable night, and as Mr Batchel felt the rain increasing to a steady drizzle he decided to abandon his walk and to return to the house by the way he had come.

He had already passed some little distance beyond the little path which descended to the Lode. The main path by which he had come was of course behind him, until he turned about to retrace his steps.

It was at the moment of turning that he had ocular demonstration of the fact that the boat had brought passengers. Not twenty yards in front of him, making their way to the water, were two men carrying some kind of burden. They had reached an open space in the path, and their forms were quite distinct: they were unusually tall men; one of them was gigantic. Mr Batchel had little doubt of their being garden thieves. Burglars, if there had been anything in the house to attract them, could have found much easier ways of removing it.

No man, even if deficient in physical courage, can see his property carried away before his eyes and make no effort to detain it. Mr Batchel was annoyed at the desertion of his terrier, who might at least have embarrassed the thieves' retreat; meanwhile he called loudly upon the men to stand, and turned upon them the feeble light of his lamp. In so doing he threw a new light not only upon the trespassers, but upon the whole transaction. No response was made to his challenge, but the men turned away their faces as if to avoid recognition, and Mr Batchel saw that the nearest of them, a burly, squareheaded man in a cassock, was wearing the tonsure. He described it as looking, in the dim, steely light of the lamp, like a crown-piece on a door-mat. Both the men, when they found themselves intercepted, hastened to deposit their burden upon the ground, and made for the boat. The burden fell upon the ground with a thud, but the bearers made no sound. They skimmed down to the Lode without seeming to tread, entered the boat in perfect silence, and shoved it off without sound or splash. It has already been explained that Mr Batchel was unable to descend to the water's edge. He ran, however, to a point of the garden which the boat must inevitably pass, and reached it just in time. The boat was moving swiftly away, and still in perfect silence. The beams of the pocket-lamp just sufficed to reach it, and afforded a parting glimpse of the tonsured giant as he gave a long shove with the sprit, and carried the boat out of sight. It shot towards the drain-pipe, then not forty yards ahead, but the men were travelling as men who knew their way to be clear.

It was by this time evident, of course, that these were no garden-thieves. The aspect of the men, and the manner of their disappearance, had given a new complexion to the adventure. Mr Batchel's heart was in his mouth, but his mind was back in the sixteenth century; and having stood still for some minutes in order to regain his composure, he returned to the path, with a view of finding out what the men had left behind.

The burden lay in the middle of the path, and the lamp was once more brought into requisition. It revealed a wooden box, covered in most parts with moss, and all glistening with moisture. The wood was so far decayed that Mr Batchel had hopes of forcing open the box with his hands; so wet and slimy was it, however, that he could obtain no hold, and he hastened to the house to procure some kind of tool. Near to the cupboard in which such things were kept was the sleeping-basket of the dog, who was closely curled inside it, and shivering violently. His master made an attempt to take him back into the garden; it would be useful, he thought, to have warning in case the boat should return. The prospect of being surprised by these large, noiseless men was not one to be regarded with comfort. Punch, however, who was usually so eager for an excursion, was now in such distress at being summoned that his master felt it cruel to persist. Having found a chisel, therefore, he returned to the garden alone. The box lay undisturbed where he had left it, and in two minutes was standing open.

The reader will hardly need to be told what it contained. At the bottom lay some heavy articles which Mr Batchel did not disturb. He saw the bases of two candlesticks. He had tried to lift the box, as it lay, by means of a chain passing through two handles in the sides, but had found it too heavy. It was by this chain that the men had been carrying it. The heavier articles, therefore, he determined to leave where they were until morning. His interest in them was small compared with that which the other contents of the box had excited, for on the top of these articles was folded 'a paynted cloth', and upon this lay the two gilded censers.

It was the discovery Mr Batchel had dreamed of for years. His excitement hardly allowed him to think of the strange manner in which it had been made. He glanced nervously around him to see whether there might be any sign of the occupants of the boat, and, seeing nothing, he placed his broad-brimmed hat upon the ground, carefully laid in it the two censers, closed the box again, and carried his treasure delicately into the house. The occurrences of the last hour have not occupied long in the telling; they occupied much longer in the happening. It was now past midnight, and Mr Batchel, after making fast the house, went at once upstairs, carrying with him the hat and its precious contents, just as he had brought it from the garden. The censers were not exactly 'black-scrap', as Mr Wardle had anticipated, or pretended to anticipate, but they were much discoloured, and very fragile. He spread a clean handkerchief upon the chest of drawers in his bedroom, and, removing the vessels with the utmost care, laid them upon it. Then after spending some minutes in admiration of their singularly beautiful form and workmanship, he could not deny himself the pleasure of calling Wardle to look.

The guest-room was close at hand. Mr Wardle, having been already disturbed by the locking up of the house, was fully awakened by the entrance of his host into the room with a candle in his hand. The look of excitement on Mr Batchel's face could not escape the observation even of a man still yawning, and Mr Wardle at once exclaimed 'What's up?'

'I have got them,' said Mr Batchel, in a hushed voice.

His guest, who had forgotten all about the censers, began by interpreting 'them' to mean a nervous disorder that is plural by nature, and so was full of sympathy and counsel. When, however, his host had made him understand the facts, he became merely impatient.

'Won't you come and look?' said Mr Batchel.

'Not I,' said Wardle, 'I shall do where I am.'

'They are in excellent preservation,' said Mr Batchel.

'Then they will keep till morning,' was the answer.

'But just come and tell me what you think of them,' said Mr Batchel, making a last attempt.

'I could tell you what I think of them,' answered Wardle, 'without leaving my bed, which I have no intention of leaving; but I have to leave Stoneground tomorrow, and I don't want to hurt your feelings, so "Good-night." Upon this, he turned over in bed and gave a loud snore, which Mr Batchel accepted as a manifesto. He has never ceased to regret that he did not compel his guest to see the censers, but he did not then foresee the sore need he would have of a witness. He answered his friend's good-night, and returned to his own room. Once more he admired the two censers as their graceful outlines stood out, sharp and clear, against the white handkerchief, and having done this, he was soon in bed and asleep. To the men in the boat he had not given another thought, since he became possessed of the box they had left behind; of the other contents of the box he had thought as little, since he had secured the chief treasures of which he had been so long in search.

Now, Mr Wardle, when he arose in the morning, felt somewhat ashamed of his surliness of the preceding night. His repudiation of all interest in the censers had not been quite sincere, for beneath his affectation of unconcern there lay a genuine curiosity about his friend's discovery. Before he had finished dressing, therefore, he crossed over into Mr Batchel's room. The censers, to his surprise, were nowhere to be seen. His host, less to his surprise, was still fast asleep. Mr Wardle opened the drawers, one by one, in search of the censers, but the drawers proved to be all quite full of clothing. He looked with no more success into every other place where they might have been bestowed. His mind was always ready with a grotesque idea. 'Blest if he hasn't taken them to bed with him,' he said aloud, and at the sound of his voice Mr Batchel awoke.

His eyes, as soon as they were open, turned to the chest of drawers; and what he saw there, or rather, what he failed to see, caused him, without more ado, to leap out of bed.

'What have you done with them?' he cried out.

The serious alarm of Mr Batchel was so evident as to check the facetious reply which Wardle was about to frame. He contented himself with saying that he had not touched or seen the things.

'Where are they?' again cried Mr Batchel, ignoring the disclaimer. 'You ought not to have touched them, they will not bear handling. Where are they?'

Mr Wardle turned away in disgust. 'I expect,' he said, 'they're where they've been this three hundred and fifty years.' Upon that he returned to his room, and went on with his dressing.

Mr Batchel immediately followed him, and looked eagerly round the room. He proceeded to open drawers, and to search, in a frenzied manner, in every possible, and in many an impossible, place of concealment. His distress was so patent that his friend soon ceased to trifle with it. By a few minutes serious conversation he made it clear that there had been no practical joking, and Mr Batchel returned to his room in tears. 'Look here, Batchel,' said Mr Wardle as he left, 'you want a holiday.'

Within a few minutes Mr Batchel returned fully dressed. 'You seem to think, Wardle,' he said, 'that I have been dreaming about these censers. Come out into the garden and let me show you the box and the other things.'

Mr Wardle was quite willing to assent to anything, if only out of pity, and the two went together into the garden, Mr Batchel leading the way. Going at a great pace, they soon came to the path upon which the box had lain. The marks it had left upon the soft gravel were plain enough, and Mr Batchel eagerly appealed to his friend to notice them. Of the box and its contents, however, there was no other trace. The whole adventure was described—the strange behaviour and subsequent flight of the terrier—the men with averted faces—the boat—and the opening of the box. Mr Batchel tried to shake the obvious incredulity of his guest by pointing to the chisel which still lay beside the path. Mr Wardle only replied, 'You want a holiday, Batchel! Let's go in to breakfast.'

Breakfast on that morning was not the cheerful meal it was wont to be. During the few minutes of waiting for it Mr Batchel stood at the window of his dining-room looking out upon the site of the well which the gardener had now covered in. He rehearsed the whole of the adventure from first to last, wondering whether the new place of safety would ever be discovered. But he said no more to his guest; his heart was too full.

The two breakfasted almost in silence, and the meal was scarcely over when the cab arrived to take Mr Wardle to his train. Mr Batchel bade him farewell, and saw him depart with genuine regret; he was returning sadly into the house when he heard his name called. It was Wardle, leaning out of the window of his cab as it drove away, and waving his hand, 'Batchel', he cried again, 'mind you take a holiday.'

THE KIRK SPOOK

BEFORE many years have passed it will be hard to find a person who has ever seen a parish clerk. The parish clerk is all but extinct. Our grandfathers knew him well—an oldish, clean-shaven man, who looked as if he had never been young, who dressed in rusty black, bestowed upon him, as often as not, by the rector, and who usually wore a white tie on Sundays, out of respect for the seriousness of his office. He it was who laid out the rector's robes, and helped him to put them on; who found the places in the large Bible and Prayer Book, and indicated them by means of decorous silken bookmarkers; who lighted and snuffed the candles in the pulpit and desk, and attended to the little stove in the squire's pew; who ran busily about, in short, during the quarter-hour which preceded Divine Service, doing a hundred little things, with all the activity, and much of the appearance, of a beetle.

Just such a one was Caleb Dean, who was clerk of Stoneground in the days of William IV. Small in stature, he possessed a voice which Nature seemed to have meant for a giant, and in the discharge of his duties he had a dignity of manner disproportionate even to his voice. No one was afraid to sing when he led the Psalm, so certain was it that no other voice could be noticed, and the gracious condescension with which he received his meagre fees would have been ample acknowledgement of double their amount.

Man, however, cannot live by dignity alone, and Caleb was glad enough to be sexton as well as clerk, and to undertake any other duties by which he might add to his modest income. He kept the churchyard tidy, trimmed the lamps, chimed the bells, taught the choir their simple tunes, turned the barrel of the organ, and managed the stoves.

It was this last duty in particular, which took him into church 'last thing', as he used to call it, on Saturday night. There were people in those days, and may be some in these, whom nothing would induce to enter a church at midnight; Caleb, however, was so much at home there that all hours were alike to him. He was never an early man on Saturdays. His wife, who insisted upon sitting up for him, would often knit her way into Sunday before he appeared, and even then would find it hard to get him to bed. Caleb, in fact, when off duty, was a genial little fellow; he had many friends, and on Saturday evenings he knew where to find them.

It was not, therefore, until the evening was spent that he went to make up his fires; and his voice, which served for other singing than that of Psalms, could usually be heard, within a little of midnight, beguiling the way to church with snatches of convivial songs. Many a belated traveller, homeward bound, would envy him his spirits, but no one envied him his duties. Even such as walked with him to the neighbourhood of the churchyard would bid him 'Good-night' whilst still a long way from the gate. They would see him disappear into the gloom amongst the graves, and shudder as they turned homewards.

Caleb, meanwhile, was perfectly content. He knew every stone in the path; long practice enabled him, even on the darkest night, to thrust his huge key into the lock at the first attempt, and on the night we are about to describe—it had come to Mr Batchel from an old man who heard it from Caleb's lips—he did it with a feeling of unusual cheerfulness and contentment.

Caleb always locked himself in. A prank had once been played upon him, which had greatly wounded his dignity; and though it had been no midnight prank, he had taken care, ever since, to have the church to himself. He locked the door, therefore, as usual, on the night we speak of, and made his way to the stove. He used no candle. He opened the little iron door of the stove, and obtained sufficient light to show him the fuel he had laid in readiness; then, when he had made up his fire, he closed this door again, and left the church in darkness. He never could say what induced him upon this occasion to remain there after his task was done. He knew that his wife was sitting up, as usual, and that, as usual, he would have to hear what she had to say. Yet, instead of making his way home, he sat down in the corner of the nearest seat. He supposed that he must have felt tired, but had no distinct recollection of it.

The church was not absolutely dark. Caleb remembered that he could make out the outlines of the windows, and that through the window nearest to him he saw a few stars. After his eyes had grown accustomed to the gloom he could see the lines of the seats taking shape in the darkness, and he had not long sat there before he could dimly see everything there was. At last he began to distinguish where books lay upon the shelf in front of him. And then he closed his eyes. He does not admit having fallen asleep, even for a moment. But the seat was restful, the neighbouring stove was growing warm, he had been through a long and joyous evening, and it was natural that he should at least close his eyes.

He insisted that it was only for a moment. Something, he could not say what, caused him to open his eyes again immediately. The closing of them seemed to have improved what may be called his dark sight. He saw everything in the church quite distinctly, in a sort of grey light. The pulpit stood out, large and bulky, in front. Beyond that, he passed his eyes along the four windows on the north side of the church. He looked again at the stars, still visible through the nearest window on his left hand as he was sitting. From that, his eyes fell to the further end of the seat in front of him, where he could even see a faint gleam of polished wood. He traced this gleam to the middle of the seat, until it disappeared in black shadow, and upon that his eye passed on to the seat he was in, and there he saw a man sitting beside him.

Caleb described the man very clearly. He was, he said, a pale, old-fashioned looking man, with something very churchy about him. Reasoning also with great clearness, he said that the stranger had not come into the church either with him or after him, and that therefore he must have been there before him. And in that case, seeing that the church had been locked since two in the afternoon, the stranger must have been there for a considerable time.

Caleb was puzzled; turning therefore, to the stranger, he asked 'How long have you been here?'

The stranger answered at once 'Six hundred years.'

'Oh! come!' said Caleb.

'Come where?' said the stranger.

'Well, if you come to that, come out,' said Caleb.

'I wish I could,' said the stranger, and heaved a great sigh.

'What's to prevent you?' said Caleb. 'There's the door, and here's the key.'

'That's it,' said the other.

'Of course it is,' said Caleb. 'Come along.'

With that he proceeded to take the stranger by the sleeve, and then it was that he says you might have knocked him down with a feather. His hand went right into the place where the sleeve seemed to be, and Caleb distinctly saw two of the stranger's buttons on the top of his own knuckles.

He hastily withdrew his hand, which began to feel icy cold, and sat still, not knowing what to say next. He found that the stranger was gently chuckling with laughter, and this annoyed him.

'What are you laughing at?' he enquired peevishly.

'It's not funny enough for two,' answered the other.

'Who are you, anyhow?' said Caleb.

'I am the kirk spook,' was the reply.

Now Caleb had not the least notion what a 'kirk spook' was. He was not willing to admit his ignorance, but his curiosity was too much for his pride, and he asked for information.

'Every church has a spook,' said the stranger, 'and I am the spook of this one.'

'Oh,' said Caleb, 'I've been about this church a many years, but I've never seen you before.'

'That,' said the spook, 'is because you've always been moving about. I'm flimsy—very flimsy indeed—and I can only keep myself together when everything is quite still.'

'Well,' said Caleb, 'you've got your chance now. What are you going to do with it?'

'I want to go out,' said the spook, 'I'm tired of this church, and I've been alone for six hundred years. It's a long time.'

'It does seem rather a long time,' said Caleb, 'but why don't you go if you want to? There's three doors.'

'That's just it,' said the spook, 'They keep me in.'

'What?' said Caleb, 'when they're open.'

'Open or shut,' said the spook, 'it's all one.'

'Well, then,' said Caleb, 'what about the windows?'

'Every bit as bad,' said the spook, 'They're all pointed.'

Caleb felt out of his depth. Open doors and windows that kept a person in—if it was a person—seemed to want a little understanding. And the flimsier the person, too, the easier it ought to be for him to go where he wanted. Also, what could it matter whether they were pointed to not?

The latter question was the one which Caleb asked first.

'Six hundred years ago,' said the Spook, 'all arches were made round, and when these pointed things came in I cursed them. I hate new-fangled things.'

'That wouldn't hurt them much,' said Caleb.

'I said I would never go under one of them,' said the spook.

'That would matter more to you than to them,' said Caleb.

'It does,' said the spook, with another great sigh.

'But you could easily change your mind,' said Caleb.

'I was tied to it,' said the spook, 'I was told that I never more should go under one of them, whether I would or not.'

'Some people will tell you anything,' answered Caleb.

'It was a Bishop,' explained the spook.

'Ah!' said Caleb, 'that's different, of course.'

The spook told Caleb how often he had tried to go under the pointed arches, sometimes of the doors, sometimes of the windows, and how a stream of wind always struck him from the point of the arch, and drifted him back into the church. He had long given up trying.

'You should have been outside,' said Caleb, 'before they built the last door.'

'It was my church,' said the spook, 'and I was too proud to leave.'

Caleb began to sympathize with the spook. He had a pride in the church himself, and disliked even to hear another person say Amen before him. He also began to be a little jealous of this stranger who had been six hundred years in possession of the church in which Caleb had believed himself, under the vicar, to be master. And he began to plot.

'Why do you want to get out?' he asked.

'I'm no use here,' was the reply, 'I don't get enough to do to keep myself warm. And I know there are scores of churches now without any kirk-spooks at all. I can hear their cheap little bells dinging every Sunday.'

'There's very few bells hereabouts,' said Caleb.

'There's no hereabouts for spooks,' said the other. 'We can hear any distance you like.'

'But what good are you at all?' said Caleb.

'Good!' said the spook. 'Don't we secure proper respect for churches, especially after dark? A church would be like any other place if it wasn't for us. You must know that.'

'Well, then,' said Caleb, 'you're no good here. This church is all right. What will you give me to let you out?'

'Can you do it?' asked the spook.

'What will you give me?' said Caleb.

'I'll say a good word for you amongst the spooks,' said the other.

'What good will that do me?' said Caleb.

'A good word never did anybody any harm yet,' answered the spook.

'Very well then, come along,' said Caleb.

'Gently then,' said the spook; 'don't make a draught.'

'Not yet,' said Caleb, and he drew the spook very carefully (as one takes a vessel quite full of water) from the seat.

'I can't go under pointed arches,' cried the spook, as Caleb moved off.

'Nobody wants you to,' said Caleb. 'Keep close to me.'

He led the spook down the aisle to the angle of the wall where a small iron shutter covered an opening into the flue. It was used by the chimney sweep alone, but Caleb had another use for it now. Calling to the spook to keep close, he suddenly removed the shutter.

The fires were by this time burning briskly. There was a strong up-draught as the shutter was removed. Caleb felt something rush across his face, and heard a cheerful laugh away up in the chimney. Then he knew that he was alone. He replaced the shutter, gave another look at his stoves, took the keys, and made his way home.

He found his wife asleep in her chair, sat down and took off his boots, and awakened her by throwing them across the kitchen.

'I've been wondering when you'd wake,' he said.

'What?' she said, 'Have you been in long?'

'Look at the clock,' said Caleb. 'Half after twelve.'

'My gracious,' said his wife. 'Let's be off to bed.'

'Did you tell her about the spook?' he was naturally asked.

'Not I,' said Caleb. 'You knew what she'd say. Same as she always does of a Saturday night.'

This fable Mr Batchel related with reluctance. His attitude towards it was wholly deprecatory. Psychic phenomena, he said, lay outside the province of the mere humourist, and the levity with which they had been treated was largely responsible for the presumptuous materialism of the age.

He said more, as he warmed to the subject, than can here be repeated. The reader of the foregoing tales, however, will be interested to know that Mr Batchel's own attitude was one of humble curiosity. He refused even to guess why the *revenant* was sometimes invisible, and at other times partly or wholly visible; sometimes capable of using physical force, and at other times powerless. He knew that they had their periods, and that was all.

There is room, he said, for the romancer in these matters; but for the humourist, none. Romance was the play of intelligence about the confines of truth. The invisible world, like the visible, must have its romancers, its explorers, and its interpreters; but the time of the last was not yet come.

Criticism, he observed in conclusion, was wholesome and necessary. But of the idle and mischievous remarks which were wont to pose as criticism, he held none in so much contempt as the cheap and irrational POOH-POOH.

MORE STONEGROUND GHOST TALES

By David Rowlands

FROM THE DIGGINGS

He brought me out of the pit;
Out of the mire and clay.
Psalm 40 v.2

What powerful spell awake to keep
That careworn Man from his needful sleep!

. . . In a closet hard by,
On his truckle bed lieth a little foot page,
A boy who's uncommonly sharp of his age.
R.H. Barham
'The Hand of Glory', The Ingoldsby Legends

FROM what has gone before, the reader will be familiar with the gravelly parish of Stoneground, its church with attendant vicarage and vicar. He will also have gathered that the present incumbent, the Revd Roland Batchel, is a man somewhat set in his ways, who none the less tends to a belief that any indigenous ghost should play a reactionary role in the daily round of so ancient a settlement.

Whereas the surrounding clays have yielded their due of fossil reptiles, the gravel has been excavated less in the cause of zoology than of profit and the Great Eastern Railway. It is an indisputable fact, however, that these sordid delvings, which have done so much to give the parish its unlovely character, have themselves yielded archaeological and zoological spoil on occasion. This may be seen in museums throughout the country, in private collections and—in one particular instance—perhaps in the library of the vicarage of Stoneground.

Despite his dislike of the diggings it is not to be supposed that Mr Batchel missed any opportunity of inspecting a new working, such as that he encountered on his round of the parish one day about the turn of the century. Excavation then was on a small scale, because of the lack of mechanical aids, and manual labour—both local and imported—was used to the full.

Thus Mr Batchel was to be found at gaze, viewing the activity with mixed feelings. These resolved into a modicum of excitement when one of the navvies—a parishioner—handed him a rusty metal object; less from devotion to the cause of archaeology than from desire for a rest and because 'his reverence' was reputed to tip well.

It was indeed a *find* and Mr Batchel seized the crumbling object with little regard for the dignity of his Office...until he realized how brittle it was. One of the advantages of gravel is that there is little dirt to be cleaned from such objects, and with trembling fingers Mr Batchel soon realized that he held an antique bronze spearhead or dagger. He was soon retreating to his vicarage, leaving old Blackett the satisfied recipient of more modern metals.

From his gardener Mr Batchel obtained an old brush, and some lamp paraffin and cleaned up the fragile object as best he could, without further damage.

The vicarage library was situated upstairs, next to Mr Batchel's bedroom as already related, and its contents were antique rather than erudite. Within his means, however, Mr Batchel had added to it from time to time, following the example of his predecessors in office.

Now the object lay on a card at his elbow, while Mr Batchel consulted his reference works. Yes, he could be fairly certain that 'he' had unearthed a veritable Anglo-Saxon dagger.

The inaccuracy of this personal pronoun did not concern him too closely. He was already planning the opening paragraph of the paper he would write to the *Archaeological Review*. 'That', he thought pleasantly to himself, 'will be one in the eye for my friend Mr Wardle, after his unkind remarks about the dinosaur footprint.'

So far in these tales the reader will have found that Mr Batchel's domestic arrangements are taken very much for granted. Indeed it may come as a surprise to learn that there was a housekeeper-cum-cook 'living in'—a respectable widow of remarkable aspect, whose son acted as house-boy: answering the door to callers, running errands, cleaning boots; and who could, by his natural instincts, be relied upon to keep the gardener up to the mark.

As has been remarked elsewhere, Mr Batchel was a great respecter of the ingenuity and inventiveness of his younger parishioners and had made strenuous attempts to confine their activities to certain clubs over which he presided. He was well aware from the kitchen accounts that this particular young limb had a voracious appetite and he was reluctantly beginning to attribute certain deficiencies in the biscuit barrel kept in the library to the same appetite. However he was a fair man and did not wish to reprimand the boy simply on suspicion.

That evening he was entertaining to dinner young Mr Groves, a clergyman from the nearby Minster precincts. In the course of the after-dinner pipe, Mr Batchel mentioned the archaeological find and took Mr Groves up to the library to see the precious object.

It will doubtless be remembered that Mr Groves was a keen amateur photographer and he offered to take a photograph suitable for illustrating the forthcoming article. This was immediately accepted by Mr Batchel who absently proffered the biscuit barrel. The paucity of the contents reminded him of his grievance and he half-jocularly related his suspicions to Mr Groves.

That gentleman chuckled. 'I can easily prove if it *is* the young rascal', he said, 'simply by setting up my flashpowder and camera to take a picture in the dark, when the library door is opened.'

To do him justice, Mr Batchel was not sure that he liked the idea . . . but in the end he agreed, feeling a certain sense of aggravation, and thinking that the sudden flash of light would probably prove more salutary a lesson than any subsequent admonition.

Accordingly, Mr Groves fetched his equipment from the Minster—ostensibly to take a photograph of the bronze dagger: which he duly did. He also left an ingenious array of wires and strings, flashpowder, lampblack and tripod to record any nocturnal visitor to the library. Mr Batchel for his part went as nonchalantly as possible to the kitchen where his staff were preparing vegetables for the morrow, and replenished the biscuit barrel.

The stage thus being set, Mr Batchel went to bed and Mr Groves returned to the Minster.

Sleep did not come readily to Mr Batchel, however. His conscience was uneasy. It suggested that he had no business to be setting traps. Despite the lad's inherent levity, he was fond enough of him to regret the thought of giving him a fright. So, after a deal of tossing and turning, he decided to 'spring the trap' himself and then return to bed, and hopefully, get some sleep.

A little topographical diversion now becomes necessary. Mr Batchel had direct access to the library from his bedroom, of course, but neither he nor Groves imagined the malefactor would enter through the vicar's bedroom. No, he would use the door from the landing outside and the flash device had been set accordingly. So, Mr Batchel put on his slippers and went out on to the landing and to the library door.

Even though he was expecting the flash, it came as a blinding shock for a moment. But it was not this which exercised his mind—far from it. The lightning flash had illuminated the library for only an instant, but quite long enough for Mr Batchel to see the stunted skeletal figure that was between himself and the camera, picking up the bronze dagger from the table. Luckily his legs still functioned, although he was not quite so sure about his heart, and he beat a quick retreat outside the door. He was in no mood to go groping around in the dark for matches to light the candle at the reading desk. Instead he got his bedside night-light, lit it and re-entered the library from his bedroom.

There were the camera, the appurtenances of the library and the table . . . but no figure, skeletal or otherwise, and—what is more (or rather, *less*)—there was no bronze dagger either.

Mr Batchel went early to the Minster and collected Mr Groves from the before-breakfast Celebration. The only evidence to be seen in the library was a small patch of gravel dust on the table top and on the carpet just in front of the table.

They returned to Mr Groves' lodgings with the precious camera and photographic plate, and set to work in the makeshift darkroom. The plate was rinsed with spirit to speed drying and finally they could examine the negative properly.

It showed a doorway and a gentleman framed in that doorway, dressed in rather Victorian night-attire and looking astonished . . . for his mouth was wide open; but of prehistoric nocturnal visitor there was no hint . . .

It was well for Mr Batchel that the earlier plate had been taken of his find. It sufficed for the writing of the article, which duly appeared—with illustration—in the *Archaeological Review*; but Mr Batchel has been hard put to find convincing reasons why he has been unable to accede to the reasonable request of those antiquarian colleagues who wish to examine the Stoneground dagger for themselves.

ONE MAN WENT TO MOW

O holy awful Reaper
Have mercy in the day
Thou puttest in thy sickle
And cast us not away.
W. St. Hill Bourne

MR BATCHEL sat in his study at the window overlooking the vicarage lawn, his hands placed over his ears. It was a beautiful summer afternoon and the window would normally have been open. Rather than the restful sounds of the countryside however, there came instead—and only faintly muffled—the dire clatter of a mechanical lawnmower.

Mr Batchel was undergoing an occasional and self-inflicted penance: a visit from his abrasive friend Mr Wardle. For the reader will probably recall that Mr Wardle was wont to comment gratuitously on his antiquarian friend's domestic arrangements. In fact during his previous visit he had been somewhat outspoken on the archaic methods prevailing in the gardening department.

Through previous decades, even centuries, and right up to this newly entered twentieth century, the lawns of Stoneground vicarage had been lovingly—if laboriously—tended by a succession of gardeners and their assistants plying scythes in graceful sweeping movements and keeping the ground and turf under strict control by much heavy rolling.

'What you need is waking up, Batchel', observed Mr Wardle pointedly. 'Why, one of these mowing machines will do the lawns in half the time, and only require one man too.'

Mr Batchel had quietly dissented. Mechanical progress did not in his view necessarily bring the benefits—if benefits they truly were—claimed by its advocates. He was well aware that one of the companies profiting from Mr Wardle's direction manufactured such machines.

Nevertheless when he went to meet Mr Wardle at the station on the occasion of his next visit, Mr Batchel was surprised to see his guest hail a porter and march back to the luggage van. A large and important crate was lowered gingerly to the ground and Wardle's strident voice could be heard giving instructions for delivery by horse dray to Stoneground vicarage. During the cab ride home he parried Mr Batchel's queries, though ready enough to comment briskly on any other subjects he was incautious enough to mention.

At last the delivery came, and Mr Batchel strove manfully to be pleased with the present he was receiving: a Randall's Patent—resplendent in garish shades of red and green paint that he was wont to associate with fairground equipment.

There followed—of course—the obligatory demonstration and the inevitable indignity of having to propel the machine himself at Wardle's behest. Certainly the grass was cropped with goat-like precision, the clippings were propelled into a neat canvas sack, and the rollers levelled the turf to a neat finish . . . but poor Mr Batchel was conscious only of his red face, his regrettable lapse into shirt-sleeves and the unflattering comments on his fitness that emanated from his friend. He could only hope that his house-boy was not able to witness the performance. Also the moving parts set up a fiendish clatter that made his head sing confusedly and scattered his thoughts just as effectively as they gathered up the cuttings.

He was very relieved to give way to Mr Wardle who proceeded to push the machine briskly up and down the lawn until tea-time.

It was at this point that Mr Batchel returned to his study. He was accustomed to spend some hours of each day working at his 'History and Antiquities of the Minster Church' when not writing for antiquarian or ecclesiastical journals. Normally he spent the 'wee sma' hours' at these labours of love, but since Mr Wardle's freely expressed concern for his sanity as a result of continuous midnight oil expended on 'that rubbish', the vicar felt obliged to devote more conventional hours to his scholarly pursuits when Wardle was visiting.

Thus we behold him . . . the all-pervading clatter of the machine dispelling and dispersing the flow of his thoughts from the manuscript. He hoped faintly that the advent of his gardener on the morrow might prove a stumbling block—either through outright condemnation of the machine (which Mr Batchel's manners would not allow himself to do) or in effecting some subtle sabotage; but he was deluding himself. The gardener and Mr Wardle were old cronies—brothers of the soil, neither reluctant to blacken hands or break fingernails in the service of horticulture.

Next day the two men breakfasted amicably together as was their wont, Mr Batchel enjoying Wardle's comments on the business affairs in his newspaper. That gentleman lit a cigar and manoeuvered his host out to the stable yard, presenting his thoughts with a sweep of his hand.

'This yard looks like an auctioneers', he observed. 'All this clutter. You'll need a shed to keep that mowing machine out of the elements, you know. Ah! That one there will do! It's only full of useless clobber so far as I can see.'

The 'shed' in question was formerly a Tack Room of the stables and full of objects dear (or in some cases probably not so dear) to Mr Batchel that had been 'put away' pending further consideration. As a man who disliked sorting things out, he nevertheless knew that if left unchecked Mr Wardle would make short shrift of his treasures and pleasures. He therefore resorted to low cunning and said that he would indeed sort through the contents of the shed while Wardle was initiating the gardener into the mysteries of the mowing machine. He felt that worthy's unhurried manner could be relied upon to extend the lesson.

In truth Mr Batchel was not averse to rummaging through his accumulation. He had quite forgotten the existence of many items and was soon engrossed. Objects were coming to light that could not possibly be destroyed . . . pieces of the sounding board that had once hung like a Sword of Damocles over the pulpit (an apt simile considering the extent of the death-watch beetle incursion into the supports); a number of battered brass and pewter vases from neglected graves in the churchyard; the carved facia panel from a linen chest; some damaged or incomplete gardening implements, including a scythe that might have been used by Father Time himself; a wheelbarrow full of flower pots but lacking its wheel—which Mr Batchel now recalled should have been collected, duly repaired, from the wheelwright last year, or perhaps the year before.

He did his best to be objective in creating two piles—things to be disposed of, and things under *no* account to be disposed of—but it was apparent even to his eye that the pile of things to be kept was infinitely larger than the other, and he felt sure that Mr Wardle would not commend his efforts. As if to resolve this speculation that gentleman appeared.

'How's it going, Batchel? Oh, good man . . . all this clutter to go, eh?' He pounced unerringly on Mr Batchel's treasures, but was soon disabused of this notion.

'The trouble is that you *want* to live in a junk yard', he retorted, rooting about with fearful energy and contriving—do not ask me how—to fix a makeshift wheel to the barrow. This he used to transport Mr Batchel's paltry discards to the rear of the stables where he set-to building a bonfire.

Meanwhile the gardener plodded slowly into view, gingerly pushing the machine across the lawn and occasionally peering into the sack to savour the miracle of the collected cuttings. He accepted the presence of 'his reverence' outside the shed and beside a promising heap of junk as a legitimate diversion, and so diverted.

'Why that be my Dad's old scythe,' he commented. 'I remembers it well. Lookee to his mark on the handle.' He swung it tentatively and a part of the handle disintegrated.

'Put it on the barrow', commanded Wardle, re-appearing and putting the order into effect himself, for the gardener was by then too engrossed in the stack to bother about the scythe. He was tugging free a dry and dusty leather jacket.

'That be my old Dad's too. Wot I lost a two-year back.' Mr Batchel could not account for its presence there other than by the supposition that the gardener had retired to the shed for a quiet siesta or a pipe of tobacco at some time in the past when he should have been toiling, and had been disturbed in his reverie. The jacket was very disreputable and beetle grubs had attacked the leather with a will. His interest in how the hide beetles had got there was short-lived for Mr Wardle grabbed it and added it to his barrowload. Mr Batchel reflected wryly that the 'Old Chap' would not have stood for the incursion of a 'Randall Patent'.

The gardener returned to his mowing while Mr Wardle wheeled his haul to the bonfire and tipped it on. The old jacket began to smoulder sullenly as it damped the flames, giving off clouds of pungent smoke.

Mr Wardle went into the shed to assess the space now available leaving Mr Batchel standing pensively beside the bonfire. The gardener tottered up with the full sack of grass cuttings.

'What'lloido with these?' he asked. Normally he made small ricks from the swept-up scythings which tended to be long stems rather than clippings. His answer came in a most peculiar fashion.

The smoke from his old Dad's jacket had spiralled unnoticed by the two men, creating a rather intense vortex. Conscious of a strange sucking noise from the fire, they turned to see a well-defined smoke spout hovering over them. More than anything it reminded Mr Batchel of a picture of Aladdin's Geenie in a long-lost picture book from his childhood. The gardener on the other hand gave vent to a regrettable 'Lor'!'

The sucking sound grew louder and they became aware of the wind streaming past them and into the fire. A stream of grass cuttings were drawn, as if by magic, from the open sack that the gardener had dropped in alarm, and they now funnelled upward into the smoke cloud. This had become a figure—or at least the upper-half—of a man; thin and elastic in proportion, clothed entirely in green grass cuttings: a truly alarming spectacle, which now reminded Mr Batchel more forcibly of Dore's 'Grim Reaper' for it appeared to brandish a scythe.

It lunged forward out of the fire and Mr Batchel was bowled over, as by a mighty wind, to sit heavily and breathlessly in the dust of the yard.

Mr Wardle emerged from the shed in time to see a minor miracle. The gardener's arthritis normally formed a favourite topic of conversation or excuse with that worthy, yet here he was literally fleeing across the lawn! He was closely followed, at about shoulder height, by what seemed to be a large green kite which swooped and dipped in pursuit as if riding against the wind. It had no strings though and seemed to be decreasing in size every moment by fragmenting into shreds of what later examination showed to be burned grass cuttings. As Wardle watched, the gardener gained the sanctuary of the shrubbery and the 'kite' finally disintegrated and vanished.

Mr Wardle helped his clerical friend to his feet—he was still gasping and blessing his soul—and they saw that the bonfire had fallen-in, the old jacket and scythe handle consumed. As they poked the remains into a shower of sparks the gardener was cautiously emerging from the shrubbery, wiping his brow. That person said nothing (for a wonder) but received the vicar's handclasp —which clinked suggestively—with some enthusiasm, for the alehouse would soon be open—and the instruction not to return until the morrow with some pleasure.

'Well, what was all that about?', demanded the irascible Wardle. Mr Batchel thought he knew only too well what it was about, but had difficulty in putting it into words for his sceptical friend, who none the less responded with less than his usual acerbity.

'I've said it before, and I'll say it again. You need a holiday, Batchel. Get away from this place for a while. Being cooped up in this parish year-in, year-out has affected your wits.'

However he did not suggest a return to the shed-clearance and was quite non-committal about further use of the mowing machine once it was installed therein. Even when the gardener reported next day that the chain which linked the rollers to the driving blades had quite unaccountably become lost, he merely remarked that possibly it had parted during the mowing and fallen among the grasses; perhaps they might find it when they next scythed the lawn against the autumn growth.

Mr Batchel had almost forgotten the strange apparition to which he owed the ensuing peace and quiet in the excitement of his discovery among the collected objects from the shed, of a pair of large iron hooks attached to rusty chains and iron-clad wooden handles. . . he surmised that they were for hitching to a horse team, and intended for the removal of burning thatch from rick or roof. He knew of no better specimens—he told the resigned Wardle—and was already planning an article for the *County Gazette*.

ONE GOOD TURN...

Non sono animabvs mortvorvm
sed avribvs viventivm*

Non clamor sed amor
cantat in avre Dei†

(Inscriptions on the 5th and 6th bells,
Stoneground parish church)

THE parish church of Stoneground had a ring of six bells of no particular merit. Indeed the vicar, Mr Batchel, was wont to remark that the Founders had been notable for their drainpipes and cisterns and that the tone of Stoneground Tenor was identical with these utilitarian castings.

The bellringers met to practise for their Sunday ringing on each Tuesday and the vicar always tried to be present; for it had not always been so.

When he had first come to the parish the ringers were a rough and ungodly lot, ringing for weddings or for paid secular occasions, but seldom on Sundays. Now it is true that Mr Batchel could have sacked them and started afresh but in his view this

* I sound not for the souls of the dead but for the ears of the living.
† The sound that reaches God above is not a clang but voice of love.

was neither charitable nor sensible. Instead, by dint of great patience and a real endeavour to get to know the individuals, he gradually won them round from old habits and to thinking of their role in the life of the church. True, many of them still did not attend Sunday services after ringing, but some did; and they all—save one of whom more anon—came to the annual 'Ringers' Service'.

Mr Batchel had one advantage over previous incumbents in that he was himself a ringer, having learned as a youngster. He had shown no great interest in the art and science of change-ringing until his university days, but by then theological colleges were well aware of the practical impact ringing clergy such as F.E. Robinson were having in reforming the exercise. Ringing guilds were evolving and winds of change—for the better—were blowing through the belfry louvres of the country. Candidates for Holy Orders were encouraged to continue with their ringing and at Cambridge Mr Batchel found every inducement to further his natural ability as a conductor.

He had taken up residence at the vicarage and found the ringers prepared for battle, awaiting his first attempt to evict them. Instead he joined them in their ringing, put right some of their mistakes and goaded them into attempting more advanced methods; thus administering what amounted to a knock-out blow in the first round. He also had old college friends at the Minster, and was able to introduce several of his local band to the delights of ten and twelve bell-ringing.

Only one diehard stuck out against these gentle endeavours. Old Tom Thrapston had been Foreman of the Ringers for forty years and was not prepared to join the ringing on Sundays. Though Mr Batchel was careful to avoid a head-on collision, it took all his tact and patience not to do so. But he was cheered by the increasing support from his ringers (as he was now able to regard them) who were keen to learn Stedman's Principle and to progress from Treble Bob simple to Surprise and Delight methods. He knew, too, that the impetus 'To show the Parson' would soon lose headway and that the practice night would revert to an old mens' gossip club. . . but no harm for that. Old Charlie Hinkins (the undertaker) could hold forth a potted history of anyone who had recently died, and there were always reminiscences of the 'old days' which Mr Batchel as a newcomer found fascinating—particularly when they touched on the Napoleonic era and the settlement of French prisoners in the area to work the brickfields.

No-one could have been more surprised than was Mr Batchel late one spring evening when there was a knock at the door and his house-boy announced (with popping eyes) 'Mr Thrapston'.

Mr Batchel bade his unexpected visitor welcome and urged him to a seat. Mr Thrapston's manner was brusque and yet embarrassed.

'I'm sorely in troubles, Reverend, and I'm come a-seeking help.'

This was the sort of appeal bound to rouse Mr Batchel. He was concerned to help, be the needy one bird or beast; man, woman or child; old or young; rich or poor. He knew from village gossip that Thrapston's wife Mary was ill. In fact he had attempted to call on her, but the old man (who had no religion himself) had refused entry, saying that his wife—who was of the French settlement stock—was a Roman Catholic and wanted no truck with Apostates!

But Mr Thrapston was continuing. . .

'The wife's a-dying and needs a priest. I went to her Roman priest in town, but he's out on another visit. Will you come?'

'Of course I will, my dear fellow,' replied Mr Batchel, 'but your wife may not accept me, you know. Our priests are not recognised by her church.'

'I don't care anyways about that, Reverend. That's for parsons. Her's a-dyin' and I don't think she'll be knowin'. But she wunnt die easy unless there's a priest to say her the words'.

While he hunted out his Communion vessels and put them into his bag, Mr Batchel swiftly reviewed his dilemma. It all seemed simple enough to Thrapston, no doubt . . . but there, the man was in trouble: what else could he do but go along? And yet he was anxious. How far could he go along the path of deluding the dying woman that he was a priest of her persuasion? He knew the ritual, of course—would he be justified in the deception?

At any rate Mr Batchel was not a man to haver and waver and as it happened the matter was largely taken out of his hands. He followed on Thrapston's heels to the house where they found the poor woman far gone and sinking. She rallied from unconsciousness, however, and seemed to be seeking comfort. So, putting aside his scruples, Mr Batchel heard her confession—Thrapston having absented himself as if on cue—and gave her absolution and her own rosary to hold. Then he spoke the Blessing and sat a moment with her before calling in the old man. He asked if he should wait but Thrapston shook his head and Mr Batchel left him seated at the bedside holding his wife's hand. The unmarried daughter showed him out.

The vicar was not one to brood unduly and so, finding himself rather restless, adjourned to the library where he read and wrote a little until morning.

At breakfast he had a message that Mrs Thrapston had died about an hour after his visit.

He was not entirely surprised to receive a visit later in the day from the Catholic priest from the nearby town; and a very angry priest at that!

This is no place for a theological diatribe on the validity of Anglican Orders, particularly since Mr Batchel was placidly detatched about the dogmatic claims of the 'Other Lot', as he termed the Roman Catholic Church. Moreover he was anxious to conclude the interview as speedily as was compatible with good manners, for he could see the gardener through his study window, clearly in need of direction. So he forbore to comment on the Father's claim that he, Batchel, had endangered the woman's soul. His own beliefs were robust enough to pooh-pooh the notion of special rights and privilege tickets as a passport to the hereafter. Sincerity was everything to Mr Batchel. So long as his action had not caused the priest to make difficulties about the burial of Mary Thrapston in the cemetery, he was content to leave the matter be.

At long last Father Toomey had finished, and Mr Batchel was able to escape to the garden and to remonstrate with the gardener about his attempts to weed the path. Mr Batchel liked weeds and admired their random tenacity. He was just in time to save some ragwort of which he had become rather fond.

Mr Batchel's amiable security received rather a jolt on the Sunday evening following. He had just finished supper and was drawing up to his fire (for the evenings were still chilly) when the boy announced old Mr Thrapston.

Having seated himself, the old gentleman seemed to find difficulty in broaching what was on his mind, and Mr Batchel had commenced some remark about the chilly evenings, when his visitor suddenly interrupted with a burst of words.

'What causes ghosts, Reverend?'

Naturally Mr Batchel was somewhat nonplussed at this direct yet unspecific query; he made some non-committal noises and asked the reason for the question, as most of us would do.

'It's Mary. She's come back, Reverend, and is a-botherin' me.'

Mr Batchel felt a sudden twinge of doubt, as if a pin had stuck into his stomach. Could the Roman priest have been right? Could the dead lady not rest?

From Thrapston's account he had woken in the early hours of Sunday to find the form of his wife at his bedside—in her night-attire as she had died—looking at him reproachfully (or so it seemed). He had asked what she wanted, but the form had not answered, just pointed vaguely to the corner of the room, before giving another accusing look and vanishing. Thrapston had puzzled over the occurrence for a while and then gone back to sleep.

He was woken—having overslept he said (though Mr Batchel was well aware that he seldom arose before midday of a Sunday)—by the sound of the bells and by hands pulling off his bedclothes. There was nothing to be seen—just the heap of bedclothes drawn to one side—and he noticed that the curtains and window had been opened. He charged his daughter with rousing him, but she denied it—saying she was too busy cooking the dinner to bother him.

He had let the incident pass until tea-time, when he'd been sitting alone at the table, his daughter having gone to the church in town. Suddenly his coat had dropped across his lap and the front door was opened. He knew it was about six o'clock for the wind blew in a gust of sound, the bells beginning to ring for service. In the dim lamp light he saw the outline of his wife fading from beside his chair, as he returned from shutting the door and hanging up his coat. She seemed to be annoyed with him, for her scowl—rather like the Cheshire Cat's grin—was the last thing he saw before she vanished.

Thrapston was now rather puzzled and had decided to come and ask the vicar's opinion—if he had any notion what she was about? Was she uneasy? Why was she not gone wherever it was the dead go?

Mr Batchel was puzzled as may be imagined. It was no time for platitudes or glib assurances, albeit well-meant. However he cannily said he would consider the matter and discuss it with Thrapston in the morning.

He saw his visitor out, preoccupied himself with trying to recall what he knew of the Catholic concept of Purgatory. Plus, of course, the nagging thought that Mary Thrapston's priest might have been right in his allegations.

Mr Batchel had intended to do some writing, but instead turned to consulting the library upstairs on thoughts about the afterlife. Although he struck on several passages that would have amused him at a different time, he found no ready comfort. He was bothered... and might as well admit it.

It must have been about two o'clock, with the library fire dwindling away and the room becoming rather cold when Mr Batchel's eye, rising from contemplation of a paragraph, was startled to see the late Mrs Thrapston standing beside him. He rubbed both eyes—she was indeed in her night-attire (insofar as Mr Batchel was able to judge of such things)—and at first his mind was exercised more by the lack of propriety shown by the lady, and what his house keeper would say were she to witness this encounter, than by the fact that this was an undoubted ghostly phenomenon.

Her smile was seraphic and her hand was raised as if in blessing however, and all the vicar's doubts and worries were erased in te next instant of beholding her. She bent forward and placed an object on the reading desk, pointing to a corner of the room and then to an opposite corner; or as Mr Batchel judged, to her own former house and to the church. Then she dissolved away, like the condensed steam on a shaving mirror, leaving him to his thoughts. On the desk was one of his set of handbells.

You may be sure Mr Batchel made the connection he would wish between the incidents, especially as Thrapston had twice been disturbed when the bells were ringing. Mary clearly wanted her husband to ring with his old friends for the services on Sundays.

In the morning—or rather the afternoon for he was nothing if not tactful—Mr Batchel made his views known to Thrapston, who had passed an uninterrupted night. Old Tom looked shrewdly at Mr Batchel with the beginning of a twinkle in his eye.

'We'll give it a try, Reverend. We'll give it a try.'

And indeed from that time onward, neither man was disturbed by any further visitation from Mary Thrapston, for Old Tom took to ringing for both services on Sundays. He could not be persuaded to attend the services, but Mr Batchel was well content, and grateful to the lady for her intervention.

If she had any other motive or intention, it has not yet been disclosed.

THE MARSH LIGHTS

An *Ignis fatuus* that bewitches
And leads men into pools and ditches
Samuel Butler

THE Great Eastern Railway runs a main line from East to West across the Northern sector of the gravelly parish of Stoneground and some of the inhabitants find their employment with that company. Although Stoneground is the penultimate station before the town, where there is a junction of lines, few trains stop there. Those that do provide a welcome means of escape from the despoilation of the diggings. Nevertheless there are portions of the parish which, although they could never be called 'beauty spots', are not without a certain melancholy attraction.

In particular there is a stretch of the railway embankment running as straight as a die eastwards, and the signal cabin close by Stoneground is quite an important outpost of the junction. From the nearby 'high ground' (a local euphemism) fine views can be obtained across the fenlands and reclaimed fields.

It was a favourite spot of Mr Batchel and in his walks around the parish—often accompanied by his terrier Punch—he would pause near the Dike and 'view the landscape o'er'. It was a fine place too for migrant birds, many of which found the telegraph wires that followed the railway a welcome resting place.

One of the signalmen, Edward Theakston, was a parishioner and shared with Mr Batchel a common interest in the wildlife of the fens, as befitted members of the Nene Natural History Society. Since both preferred observation to slaughter they were somewhat *de trop* with the majority of Society members who tended to shoot at anything which moved, thus ensuring the permanent rarity of anything unusual in the vicinity and preventing the ordinary person from being startled by the unknown.

Mr Theakston was the proud possessor of a pair of naval binocular glasses which he kept handy in the signal cabin ready to be focussed on any bird of passage or—it has to be admitted—interesting business of his fellow humans.

There was always a welcome for Mr Batchel and Punch of an afternoon or evening, should they chance by, and a cup and dish of tea respectively.

As Mr Batchel climbed the cabin steps at dusk one day, with Punch close at heel, he reflected that the cabin might be a pleasant enough place on a warm summer day when dragonflies played over the marshes, but a lonely and eerie place in the pitch dark of a winter's night.

Indeed, it was an aspect of this eerieness of the fens that currently interested the two men. For they were investigating the occasional marsh light, will o' the wisp, Jack o'Lantern . . . call it what you will.

From the Middle Ages up to more recent times many fenland churches burned a night light to show late travellers the way. By contrast the flickering lights that sometimes appeared on the marshes were supposed to be a lure of the devil to mislead the wanderer into the swamp. The question being, what were these strange lights? Were they animal or insect? Or simply luminous gas rising from the bogs?

Mr Batchel had been consulting the vicarage library and found that despite its conservative and theological origins it had a leavening of venerable science. He was thus able to quote to Mr Theakston the remarks of Derham of 1727 and even of Newton in 1730 on the subject. Both these eminent men being of the opinion that such *igniis fatui* were phosphorescent vapours.

Now Mr Batchel never took a walk about the fens at dusk or after dark without slight misgivings. Although several years had elapsed since the horrifying ordeal of his former friend and neighbour the vicar of Yaxholme, that occurrence had only just been made public.* So that when Mr Batchel first saw a light while walking after dark near the Dike, he felt it would be unwise to leave the path. However, he had with him a good, stout, walking stick, and by poking this through the reeds he was able to see the soft yellow light hovering among the frondage.

As befitted an honours graduate in the Natural Sciences Tripos, he decided to make careful examination. Muttering to himself a misquotation of Milton anent the phenomenon that 'Hovered and blazed with elusive light', he knelt and pushed the tip of his stick into what he judged to be the source. Even after many long minutes however, the metal ferrule of the stick was not warmed, nor was the stick marked in any way.

He then cut a bullrush with his penknife and trimmed it to leave a long, hollow stem. One end he pushed into the glow, the other he put to his lips and blew. The light flickered uncertainly but was not extinguished; nor could he lead off any gas that would ignite with a lucifer.

'Well, well', he said aloud; rising stiffly—warned to do so by the increasing dampness of his knees. 'Newton was right then—a cold phosphorescence it is. What causes it though? That is the question!'

At home next day he enlisted the aid of the gardener in setting up an old hip-bath into which they (the gardener that is;

* *Vide* R.H. Malden: *Between Sunset and Moonrise.*

Mr Batchel's role was directive) slurried some peaty soil, rotted leaves and some kitchen remains in which old eggshells and fish-bones featured prominently. The whole was then stirred into a sludge with buckets of muddy water from the Lode, and left in an outhouse covered with sacks to keep the light out and the malodourous vapours in.

A tube was taken from just above the surface and in a matter of days the enthusiastic Mr Batchel was able to collect, by displacing water, a gas which stank worse than the mixture and which exploded vigorously on being stimulated with a match. Despite every encouragement however—even the spectacle of a shame-faced and self-conscious clerk in Holy Orders walking widdershins round the tub and reciting 'A wandering fire, compact of unctuous vapour, which the night condenses, and the cold environs kindle through agitation to a flame'—despite, I say, all this inducement, the vapours obstinately refused to phosphoresce or to ignite themselves.

The results of this fascinating but abortive experiment Mr Batchel had communicated to Ted Theakston over a cup of tea. On that particular day, one of the linesmen gangers was present and took some interest in the conversation. He averred that he regularly saw a 'lantern' a-bobbing over Northey Fen as he walked home to Thurnley of a night. His hearers were well aware however, that this walk took place after closing time at the 'Crossed Sprits' and were not minded to give it undue credence. Their poorly concealed disbelief provoked the ganger into returning next day with a workmate who confirmed the sighting of the mysterious light.

Ted Theakston had a fen-boat; one of the short, flat bottomed punts used thereabouts, and accordingly he and Mr Batchel decided that they would take this opportunity to investigate the phenomenon at first hand.

So, a couple of nights later, they set out in the boat, as soon as Theakston was relieved from duty, with Punch in the prow and a couple of dark lanterns stowed safely at their feet.

To anyone unaccustomed to the fens, the aura of dank vegetation and the hungry midges would have been a powerful deterrent. Northey Fen was no exception and indeed Mr Batchel observed that Punch was restless and seemed to be losing his appetite for adventure, for he was now lying down and giving vent to little protesting grizzles.

The reader will not need telling that labouring at the sprit (or punting pole) and manoeuvring the boat had fallen to Ted Theakston's lot. It was perhaps appropriate, therefore, that Mr Batchel should have his attention drawn from his terrier's behaviour by being the first to spot the light. There it was in truth; a winking, bobbing, yellowish glow. As the boat was put about toward it, they were momentarily diverted—and indeed nearly upset—by Punch taking it into his head to abandon ship and, with a mournful yowl, to splash away whence they had come, homeward bent.

Mr Batchel was complacent about Punch's swimming ability and homing instinct; fortunately his complacency was subsequently justified.

The situation suddenly reminded him though of the adventure in finding (and losing again!) the long-lost church censers, vestments and candlesticks,* and he knew a quickening of excitement as the boat nosed through the reeds to ground itself on a mudheap.

The mysterious light had vanished at the first sound from Punch, and it had uncomfortably occurred to both men that they might be intruding where their presence would be resented. There had been a few local burglaries it was true, but no more than might be regarded as 'usual'. . . could this lonely fen be a hiding-place for the booty?

As they crept out of their boat a clinking was heard, and Theak-

* *Vide: The Place of Safety.*

ston unhooded the lanterns while Mr Batchel plied his electric torch. Both men cried out—Mr Batchel in particular anguish—for he recognized only too well the two gigantic, muffled figures: Johns Spayn and Gounthropp as the inventory of 1552 had named them, rising up seemingly out of the ground, bearing a sack between them before climbing into their punt and making off into the desolate wastes of the fen. Pursuit was not to be thought of; the two monks knew where they were bound, and Mr Batchel knew that present day obstacles like mud banks and reed beds would not hinder; for them this was open water.

Clearly they had no intention yet of yielding up their precious chattels—perhaps not until they felt the parish had moved back somewhat closer to Rome.

Meanwhile there was this curious mudbank in which Theakston's interest was of the slightest, but which appealed to Mr Batchel's curiosity. Why had the two ancient Edwardians picked *that* spot to hide their church treasures after their use of the vicarage well had been discovered?

Mr Batchel might be preoccupied with the sixteenth century, but Edward Theakston was a practical man, believing they should return and report to the police constable what they had seen. The vicar was in some doubt as to the welcomeness of such information as they had to lay at eleven-thirty in the evening but he saw this as the easiest way to avoid controversy and to be alone with his thoughts.

Their reception at the policeman's house was indeed tepid. That gentleman—still hastily buttoning the tunic of office around his open shirt-front—confined himself to the observation that it was 'Strordinary', and to making an entry in the official notebook with much flourishing of an indelible pencil and licking of the lead.

It took Mr Batchel three days to recruit the labourers he wanted from among the Broughtons, Lallements and Bunnums of his parish and to ensure that the policeman was planning no official investigation of Northey Fen.

After an hour or so at the digging, Mr Batchel (who was directing operations) realized that the mudbank was the site of an old oratory. Some well-decayed and muddied steps led downwards, explaining why the ghostly monks had risen progressively out of the ground. The barnack stone was badly eroded and the remains of walls indicated that they had been built of flint rubble. Any attempts to dig deeper were readily frustrated by the seeping in of water. Nothing else came to light, but Mr Batchel was well content.

He had long known of the supposed existence of this place, thought to have been dedicated to St Peter and of which the advowson had stayed with Ely until the fourteenth century. It was mentioned briefly in that inventory of 1552 as a 'Leper Chapel on Northlea Broad'—the surrounding waters providing the isolation deemed necessary—though by this time leprosy was fortunately on the decline. He smiled wryly at the thought of how safe the two ancient churchwardens must have thought their treasure would be at the leper chapel . . . now they had once again removed the objects elsewhere, and he felt considerable sympathy with their anxiety. But for their excessive zeal in revisiting the spot each night, their second hiding-place would have sufficed and the site of the chapel have remained a mystery.

Like many ponderers he spoke his thoughts out loud. 'It was pure chance, gentlemen. I shall not willingly seek your new place of safety.' He sighed. 'But I should like to know the dedication of this chapel.'

A few days later Mr Batchel spent an evening in Cambridge. Not, as might be supposed, at his old college, but with the Provost of a more illustrious foundation. Common interests in music, in drama and in the welfare of the choristers had drawn the men together when Mr Batchel had been serving his first curacy and his friend was a graduate student on the threshold of Fellowship.

A deeper interest in matters antiquarian and a not dissimilar sense of humour had kept them in touch; so they dined together once or twice a year.

Inevitably Mr Batchel was full of his discovery and the Provost thought he remembered some pertinent details in recent Ely papers sent to the Fitzwilliam. To this library they made their leisurely way after dinner (doors being open at all hours to so senior a Fellow as the Provost). Sure enough, among miscellaneous papers relating to the outstations of Ely was a description of the chapel at Northlea.

The resident priest had lived beneath the place, as was common in those days... his task being to minister to the lepers who were tended there in complete isolation. It seemed that in the later sixteenth century the chapel had been secularized and made over as a store of some kind, being only occasionally used for services. The priest's accounts itemised... '2d to carpenter for hangyng uppe ye belle and for takyng it downe agayne'... and '8d for carrienge pullpit to ye chappelle and bryngyng home agayne'. There were no subsequent records other than that James I sold the site to a private purchaser in 1608, whereafter the location became no concern of the church. Yet again there was no mention of the dedication, and this seemed destined to remain a mystery.

However when Mr Batchel returned home he received a mild shock... for there on his chest of drawers stood a small stone figure, clearly broken away—Dowsing fashion—from a church doorway or niche. It was extremely dirty and weatherworn, but his housekeeper had put out water for him to wash and that good lady must have been surprised at the amount of mud left in the bowl after Mr Batchel had gently cleansed the figure.

Many of the chisel lines had worn smooth but the figure was clearly dressed in alb, stole and chausable beneath a pallium. The chausable was cut away in a style reminiscent of the Bayeux tapestry. The hands held what appeared to be an open gospel and the inevitable keys.

For Mr Batchel this last was evidence enough of the statue and hence (he surmised) the dedication of the ancient chapel being St Peter; even had the letters 'PETR' not been crudely—*and that recently*—daubed on the back of the figurine.

This identity was accepted by the Diocesan Authorities who dated the effigy as twelth or thirteenth century and installed it in a side chapel of the nearby Minster which rejoiced in the same patronage.

The housekeeper and other servants knew nothing of the figure, but she did mention in a different context, that her son had seen a 'big fellow' in monkish dress 'hanging around' the house at twilight the previous evening.

There is seldom total agreement among any authorities however. The Provost, for example, points out the unusual clean-shaven features and tonsure, suggests that the 'key' is, in fact, a 'hand cross and orb badly weathered', and has taken great pains—via a paper in a learned journal—to demonstrate the resemblance to an eleventh-century likeness of the third Pope in a wall painting in St Clement's church, Rome.

Peter or Clement, it gives them scope for argument whenever they meet for dinner.

Mr Batchel thinks the ambiguity presented by the two ghostly Johns may be their little joke at his expense...

And he is still none the wiser about the origins of the marsh lights.

PROVIDING A FOOTNOTE

Good Ivy, say to us, what birds hast thou?
None but the Lich-Owl that cries, 'How, How'
And the Cuckow that bids wives beware.

Fifteenth-century carol

All riot eschew. Begin life anew,
And new-cushion and hassock the Family Pew!

The Lay of the Naiad
The Ingoldsby Legends

THE Ladies Working Party of St John's church Stoneground met on Monday, Wednesday and Friday afternoons and were a power in the land. For the sale of soft-furnishings, toys, clothing and other items which they made provided much money toward the very necessary repairs and upkeep of the church.

And while they industriously plied their sewing, knitting and embroidery needles, their tongues were similarly employed in discussion of their neighbours and of parish matters generally. The vicar, being both bachelor and unpractical, came in for a good deal of comment, though his occasional visits limited their opportunity for complete freedom of debate on his failings.

Mr Batchel liked to be present and also—he hoped—to encourage the ladies at work, for there was much needing monies:

the old box seats were being replaced in the aisles, the spire needed attention, a new pulpit was planned for the chancel. A new High Altar was required also—a permanent structure to replace what Mr Batchel had at first indignantly dismissed as a 'kitchen table' until he remembered the origins of The Last Supper and then felt thoroughly ashamed of himself. However this last would have to wait awhile: to his simple parishioners altars and furnishings equalled popery and they were in no mood for that!

Wandering between groups of busy ladies and girls, stopping for a word here and there, Mr Batchel sometimes overheard snatches of talk which he felt bound to ignore. Occasionally he wondered if a word in season was called for about common charity, but then he reflected that much the same topics were debated with equal malice in the belfry on Tuesdays, and if he felt no compulsion to 'put in a word' there, in or out of season, why then should he interfere where the work output and benefit to the church were so prodigious? The tongue might truly be a 'dangerous member' but it certainly lubricated the joints of the ladies' deft fingers and thumbs.

One small group of the working party were currently recovering the hassocks from the chancel pews wherein sat (on Sunday mornings only) the few gentry the parish could boast who had not sold their birthright to the Brick Company. Mr Batchel was not much concerned over this work. The majority of his people had to suffer hard wooden kneelers or the stone-flagged floor in the Nave and he felt the knees of the chancel-ites might learn a touch of welcome humility from footrests without hassocks. But Miss Oague, who ran the 'Working Party', was herself a chancel-ite and could not be expected to share these democratic sentiments.

Indeed Mr Batchel was slightly in awe of Miss Oague, who was domineering and of ample proportions. Her parents had been agent and housekeeper, then caretakers, to the Manor (which burned down in 1899) and this—in her eyes—gave her standing in the village and a right to the Manor Pew in the church. She always reminded Mr Batchel of his prep school because her attitude to him was brisk and matronal. In thundery weather he had an occasional dream from which he would start awake in nervous perspiration, in which Miss Oague proposed marriage and he could not find words to decline politely but was thereupon rushed into matrimony and a honeymoon at Eastbourne.

Among the little group of hassock re-coverers this day, he spotted Alice Bower, daughter of the organist and a great favourite of his. She seemed to be receiving admonishment from 'The Ogre', and he hastened forward... but whatever was said had been said, and although Alice addressed a rejoinder at Miss Oague's retreating back, Mr Batchel was none the wiser. However he contrived to walk home with the girl, whom he thought was unduly subdued; then, with little artfulness, to be invited into the shop parlour for tea. He hoped that there was nothing amiss with her friendship for young William Burchell, which he trusted was going to lead to an engagement soon. Perhaps she was sickening for an illness... he hoped not.

Fortunately Mrs Bower was busy in the shop and so he was able to draw Alice out a little. After much roundabout conversation Mr Batchel learned that the girl had taken a dislike to the hassock she had been re-covering. It was for Miss Oague's pew and was being refurbished with a robust square of tapestry which the lady told her was all that survived on an ancient screen destroyed in the Manor fire. Mr Batchel had not noticed the design himself, but Alice described it somewhat vehemently as 'Like nasty ivy leaves.'

Now the vicar was rather partial to ivy—despite its allegedly damaging effect on trees and buildings (which in any case he pooh-poohed as nonsense). He thought the vicarage looked well with its covering of ivy, particularly in the autumn sun when the entire walls were covered in rich red tints before the new green supervened.

'Come, Alice,' he said gently. 'Ivy is our Church's symbol of life everlasting as you know, and so it is quite appropriate for a hassock. And the family at the Manor for generations were called Ives. It is their emblem. What is called a punning device.'

By this time Alice was more herself and not to be stalled with platitudes.

'Well, sir, that's as maybe. But why does folk fear ivy then? They say it chokes trees and kills 'em'.

Mr Batchel was at pains to explain that this was folklore—ivy had roots of its own and drew its nutrients from the soil, and so on...

Alice was only half-listening and shook her head rebelliously.

'Well, anyways, I saw it *move*, Mr Batchel, sir, and... well, look you here.' She blushed and with a sudden movement pulled up the hem of her skirt and showed a pretty leg which would have delighted William Burchell, but which caused poor Mr Batchel no little embarrassment. Alice pointed out where a series of red marks ascended *round* the limb from ankle to knee, before reverting to her usual modest self. Mr Batchel wiped his forehead and coughed. 'You had better tell me all about it, child'.

It seemed that Alice had made the tapestry into a sort of slipcover for the hassock and had sat looking at the pattern of ivy leaves on the hessian backing which she was stitching up. As she stared, somewhat mesmerized, she had seen the five-pointed leaves begin to tremble. 'Like each one was a leafy hand', she pronounced.

Mr Batchel was forced to acknowledge that the leaf of the climbing ivy was five-pointed and could look rather like a membraneous hand. He rather disliked the notion and began to understand the child's aversion a little better.

Alice had finished her sewing and put the hassock down at her feet while she turned to answer some remark by her neighbour Mrs Bunnum. She became aware of something tickling her ankle and creeping up her calf to the knee. She thought it was a spider and—being a hard-headed country lass—thought nothing of it; nothing that is, until she felt *five fingers squeeze her knee*. 'I felt prickly pins and needles all down my leg, too!'

'Then,' she gulped and blushed deep red, 'It crep' right up to my hip. I stood and looked down, and it was *ivy* sir, a-growin' up out of that there hassock and up my leg. I pulled at it and kicked the hassock and it went—the ivy, sir, it just went. Then that Miss Oague came over and was a-tellin' me off for kicking her kneeler.'

Mr Batchel had also blushed at the implication of the girl's story, which he hardly liked to think about and he hoped fervently that she would not do so. Fortunately she was neither a neurotic nor an imaginative child.

'Upon my soul!' he exclaimed. 'Don't worry, Alice. I will see to it that you never have to touch the hassock again.' He changed the subject to more mundane, but interesting, topics.

'Are you going to see William tonight? Look here, try and get him to come along to the Covenanters, will you? There's a good girl.' And so on . . .

As soon as he could, Mr Batchel left the Bowers' parlour and returned to the village hall. One or two ladies were still clearing away cups and chattering over the washing-up. He asked for Miss Oague—ignoring the knowing glances that were exchanged—and found that she had just left, to take the recovered hassock to her pew in church.

To their surprise he asked a couple of ladies to accompany him there and pretended not to hear Miss Dacre's *sotto voce* remark about 'safety in numbers'.

Just as they reached the South door, a cry rang out from within the church and as they hastened inside, a distraught and dishevelled Miss Oague ran to them from the chancel.

Mr Batchel got the two ladies to take the frightened woman back to the hall for a cup of tea. He had only one question for her: 'Did you kneel on the hassock to pray?' and the poor woman stared at him and then nodded.

I fear we have to digress for a moment to describe the chancel a little.

The choir stalls were new, having been replaced in 1894, but the whole was dominated by the east window, which has already been described in these stories.* There was a fourteenth century window on the south side filled—alas—with modern glass. It was formerly a confessional window and there was a niche—nowadays enclosed by woodwork—where the priest had once sat to hear confessions of penitents outside in the churchyard. Close by this 'priest's cupboard' was the Manor Pew. And there, on the floor—lying askew—was the hassock.

Mr Batchel picked it up and looked at the tapestry cover. As Alice had said, it was a simple pattern of ivy leaves twined round what must have been the border of a larger design, probably incorporating the crest of the Ives family.

Looking hard at it he could see why the design had upset even so stolid a child as Alice—the leaves *were* like hands: like green hands with webbing between the fingers. But there was no sense of movement even though he stared at it until his eyes ached.

He weighed the hassock in his hand, he shook it by his ear: nothing to arouse comment. He even smelled it—a faint odour of old hymn books and Gothic Church of England, that was all.

He carried it out into the vestry and put it down on the deeds chest there. Rummaging in his pocket he found his pen knife—kept razor-sharp for 'mending' his quill—and with sudden decision, he cut barbarously into the cushion.

To his surprise, amongst the usual horsehair stuffing he came to an ancient canvas sack, lightly coated in pitch, but which

* *Vide: The Eastern Window.*

seemed to have retained its pliability. On cutting into this, a powerful and musty odour assailed his nose, reminding him of a fox's 'earth'. The sack was full of hair—long, thick, curly hair, and a greasy piece of parchment-like cloth with writing on it. This he could read only with difficulty:

Ye hare and ye fyngre nayles of Harald Ivyes, gent., who in lyfe dydd lusst and cuckolld and in seekying lyfe everlastyng founde deathe. Here playced by Jeffrye Smyth, clerkke to ye Vicar, 1720. Hollde hym stylle in ye Lord.

This brought considerable enlightenment to Mr Batchel. He remembered the name of Harold Ives as a libertine and evil-liver from his reading into the parish history. Unlike other Ives in the long-extant family, there was no memorial to him in the church.

He gathered up the hassock and its grisly contents and made his way carefully down the stoke-hold steps, where he pushed them into the boiler; watching with relief as the flames consumed them.

Mr Batchel then inquired after Miss Oague and found that her companion, the down-trodden Miss Ward, had fetched her home and put her to bed.

He never did learn from the lady what her experience had been and she made no inquiry about the missing hassock, being quite content with the more conventional one that replaced it. A few weeks later, she and the jubilant Miss Ward departed for a sea voyage that took them away from the parish for more than a twelvemonth.

Upstairs in the vicarage library Mr Batchel had turned to a well-thumbed and much annotated book, Giddings' *History of the Manor and Parish of Standground* (1820). He soon found the requisite entries. . . Giddings had something to say (and none of it good) of Harold Ives, culled from the parish records and a vicar's journal of the 1700s. . .

Of Harold Ivies there is naught but ill repute. In the words of his Vicar he was a 'vane and godless manne', and by all accounts a lecher and evil-doer, ruination to any woman he encountered be she maiden, goodwife or granddame. There was a saw or saying in the parish that he was kin to the ivy bush, so often did he seek its aid to climb walls, enter houses or otherways gain access to his paramours.

It is said of his end that he fell from the creeper of Mr White's house, in a stupor from 'ye herballyst's syrupps whyche (he) tooke seekyng to renewe hys mannlye powers yt hadde waynd, yt (he) myght bee eternallye sapfull' and that his crushed head and limbs were so entangled in the ivy that he strangled, for Mr White, wroth at his presence, afforded him no aid.

He was buried in North Churchyard and the ivy grew strongly from his grave and to such purpose that it would entangle any passing woman in its clutch. The Vicar took steps to contain this nuisance, but it is not recorded by what means he achieved this end.

'Hmm,' said Mr Batchel to himself, taking up his quill and dipping it.

'I think, Mr Giddings, that we are in a position to furnish you with a footnote.'

And after a moment's thought, he began to write in the margin . . .

OFF THE RECORD

or

THE RECORDING ANGEL*

A chantry fair, And of Monks a pair,
To pray for his soul for ever and aye,
Thou must duly endow, Sir Ingoldsby Bray,
And fourteen marks by the year thou must pay
For plenty of lights to burn there o'nights.

The Ingoldsby Penance

RETURNING TO THE vicarage from watching Sam Bower put the horses into the churchyard to crop the grass and weeds, Mr Batchel had received a strident 'Huloo' as a lady dismounted from her bicycle. Now it is true that Miss Wilkins smoked cigars and had a deplorable tendency to appear in public in labourer's trousers. She was also apt to forget herself and her surroundings and employ rather forceful expressions, though usually in one of the five or six languages she spoke fluently, rather than in English or French. Nevertheless Mr Batchel valued her as an 'original'; and his liking was more to do with the qualities of her mind and her discourse, than with her ancestry and hereditary distrust of the church. For Miss Wilkins' was quite the oldest family in the region, in direct descent from the de Villechins,

* In affectionate memory of Elspeth Read and of R. Tarrant-Bailey whose accounts of early recording machines and practice fascinated me.

and she was wont to propound that most of their titles and property had been sucked out of them by successive Abbots of Thorney. All documentary evidence had been destroyed at the Reformation, however, nor had restoration been made, for the Villechins were too cussed and independent to bow to monarch or prelate.

Miss Wilkins owned a house out on the Yaxholme road, well out of the village; but she was not often in residence, for she owned several other houses in England and in various other parts of the world. Being interested in science and mechanics, and gifted with her hands, she dabbled in many inventions and hobbies . . . a number of which—music and photography for instance—she shared with Mr Batchel and his younger friend Mr Groves.

Just at present, instead of drinking her tea, Miss Wilkins was on her knees, repairing the stylus arm of Mr Batchel's cherished phonograph, and reprimanding him in rather a booming voice for letting wax shavings from the cylinders get into the clockwork mechanism. Mr Batchel understood the *theory* of making recordings on wax (or cardboard come to that) but little of the actual mechanics of doing so. In fact he often thought that the working of the ingenious machine was deliberately designed to frustrate him.

Elspeth Wilkins not only repaired phonographs, she collected recording machines of all types and had devised a clockwork mechanism of her own that bore a patent, and which depended on descending weights to provide more regular and constant drive to the cylinder—and thence a less wobbly recording—than did an uncoiling mainspring. The drawback was that the performer had perforce to climb up to a platform or seat perched high in the air in order to play or sing into the recording trumpet, since the weights needed room to descend below the recording mechanism.

Mr Batchel was keen to secure a cylinder recording of his church choir singing Barnby's anthem 'It is High Time to Awake' which, thanks to his long struggles with the choirmaster, they performed quite creditably. The problem was that in the comparative vastness of the church, no matter where his recording machine was placed, only a tiny amount of sound—and that predominantly treble and Mrs Hathaway—went down the trumpet and on to the wax via the cutting stylus. A further attempt to assemble the choir within the confines of his study had only produced considerable heat and stuffiness and a discordant acoustic roar, due—as Miss Wilkins pointed out (waving her cigar emphatically)—to the blanketing effect of the study furnishings and the choir's clothing. She laughed hugely:

'Get the choir to perform without clothes on, or with just a loincloth apiece if they must be modest!'

Mr Batchel was not particularly amused by this daunting suggestion. 'It would hardly be conducive to reverence or seemliness,' he sighed, unable to repress a small smile. 'And if I suggest recording only one-third of the choir, the rest will take offence. We have only just healed matters after the discord over the Sunday School outing.'

Miss Wilkins came to his rescue:

'Can we use the vestry? And do you mind a bit of rigging?'

The vestry, which led off from the north side of the chancel through a fourteenth century doorway, was quite large. It had originally been a chantry chapel before the Reformation, under the direction of the Abbot of Thorney and more recently, before the Education Act and establishment of Board Schools, had housed the Church School. In the present, it was still used for small meetings or for choir practices in winter if attendance was small, for there was a harmonium and an open hearth with a flue (where Mr Batchel thought the chantry altar had once been) where a gas fire could be used to create some creature comfort. The men's choir robes hung there, and a door gave on to the priest's vestry, where Mr Batchel robed and kept the communion vessels and other church plate. The choir women did not robe and normally sat apart from the men in church.

Mr Batchel thought hard for a moment, and then nodded; wagging a cautionary finger at his lady friend.

'But nothing unseemly, mind.'

'Trust me,' grunted that person, rising and stubbing out her cigar butt on a shoe, before sticking it behind her ear for future reference.

During the next few days, Elspeth Wilkins could be seen striding about in the chancel of the church, much concerned with measurements around the vestry door, and a sketching pad on which she made numerous jottings. She also on occasion commandeered young Robert Blakes (that most shrill of trebles) from the village school and Mr Horton (a most *profundo* of *bassos*) from the smithy and had them singing scales until they were purple. Finally she fetched in the two Rockfords and unfolded to them a plan of what she wanted made up in sections in their workshop.

This proved to be a long and large wooden trumpet that fitted into the vestry door-frame and extended out into the church in front of the sanctuary gate, ending in a spout of a diameter that exactly fitted into the horn of Mr Batchel's recording machine.

'You see,' she confided to that intrigued gentleman, 'if you now have the choir to sing inside the vestry, you can have the harmonium accompaniment and you will all actually be performing *inside the recording trumpet*! What do you think of that, eh? It should capture all the sound, I think. My only worry is about reverberation inside the wooden section.'

'Most ingenious,' said Mr Batchel, who was indeed impressed with the idea.

'Right,' she said, 'we'll try it out then.'

So saying, she stationed Perkins, her gardener-handyman, at the recorder and marched the vicar outside and into the vestry from the churchyard door. After closing the door to the inner vestry and pulling the curtain across it, she seated herself at the harmonium, banged on the lid as a signal to Perkins, and launched into the opening chords of 'Abide With Me.' She waved her arm invitingly at the vicar to add his reedy tenor to her fruity contralto.

The impromptu duet over, they re-entered the church and detached the machine from its wooden extension. With bated breath the cylinder was carefully brushed free of loose wax shavings where the stylus had scribed its erratic course. The motor was re-wound and the recording played. To their delight a good balance had been achieved between harmonium and voices, and although Mr Batchel's somewhat faltering tones were rather swamped by the booming of his duettist, they were nevertheless audible. It all augured well for the effect with the full choir.

The recording made an agreeable opportunity for chatter and disruption of the usual choir practice, and it took rather a long time for the autocratic Miss Wilkins to push and pummel the members into place. She had them in a random scattering of voices, rather than grouping 'parts' together, hoping this would balance the recording if not the singing: for some found it distracting to have a different 'part' harmonized on either (or in some cases all four) sides of them. There was much buzz and chatter and—regrettably—a certain amount of giggling at the unusual mingling of the sexes. At last all was ready however, and after a brisk knock on the wooden trumpet wall, Miss Wilkins waved in Mr Bower at the harmonium . . . a few mellow notes, then the choirmaster—standing on a hassock—ushered in the choir's voices . . . a little hesitantly at first, but gaining confidence and strength.

To their disappointment, although the recording was acoustically well-balanced there was some reverberation from within the wooden trumpet, and an overall 'tinniness' that was not pleasant to the ear.

'Pah', said Miss Wilkins, emphatically. 'It's that rotten little machine of yours... it's only fit for talking into really. Leave it to me and I'll get my "Majestic" along.'

Mr Batchel was rather beginning to regret that he had put his original wish into words; but it was too late to draw back.

'What about the descending weights?' he asked anxiously. 'You cannot dig up the floor of the church and' (with an air of fore-stalling an obvious suggestion) 'it would be most irreverent to run them down into the crypt.'

'No problem there,' responded that determined lady. 'I'll record it from the roof, by taking the sound up the chimney flue.' She marched off briskly before Mr Batchel could make further comment.

In spite of Mr Batchel's apprehensions, Elspeth Wilkins caused little trouble, and in any case the vicar was pleased to have the unsightly wooden trumpet removed from the chancel. Her activities, indeed, were confined to getting the Rockfords and her own men to construct a temporary platform up to the level of the vestry roof, where they winched up her machine with block and tackle so that the weights could travel down to the ground and the recording horn could be linked to the chimney-pot via an ingenious papier mâché tube. The construction was not visible from the church path (only from the graveyard) and in any case was tarpaulined-over against the certainty of inclement weather. All was completed late on the Thursday evening before the choir practice on the Friday. Mr Batchel bade Miss Wilkins and her team goodnight, with some optimism for a successful recording on the morrow.

He slept fitfully, however, and after tossing and turning for some while was about to get out of bed and go into the library when his ear caught—very faintly—the sound of chanting. It was nearing Eastertide and a week of really spring-like weather had encouraged the leaving-open of windows. It seemed to the vicar that the sound was coming from below his window.

When he leaned out and looked over the churchyard wall, it was evidently coming from the church, and he even thought he could detect a faint light from the chancel, the contour of which in the darkness looked different from the accustomed aspect.

His Hunter showed that it was 3 a.m. and he pulled on a robe and thick stockings before going downstairs and out into the churchyard. As he hastened up the church path he realized that the light came not from the chancel but from the vestry on the north side. His first thought was that the outrageous Elspeth was burning midnight oil on her creation; but he slowed up, puzzled. It was a melodious male voice he could hear, chanting in a minor key and unaccompanied except by an occasional intoned response. He began to recognize the form of the medieval *Missa Brevis* just as it dawned on him that the external appearance of the vestry was considerably altered. The windows were different and glazed with plain material from which the protective netting had been removed.

On looking through into the vestry he got a profound shock—a wondrous surprise indeed, but a pleasant one to anyone so interested in the history of the parish as himself. . . for he was clearly seeing the vestry as it had been in medieval times, in use as a chantry chapel. Tapers burned on the wall and on the small stone altar, where the monk was intoning the Mass; answered by another brother—as roughly garbed—who was serving. Winking at Mr Batchel in the candlelight were a silver wafer-box and chalice, on which his eyes could just discern the Boar's Head device of the de Villechin family!

The exterior door had vanished, though this was not surprising in view of the regression of time that seemed to have occurred on the site. Instead Mr Batchel tried the north door, which he knew had been closed since the early nineteenth century. He entered thereby, noting with a nod of satisfaction the absence of the familiar organ . . . but he was unable to enter the chantry because of the screen, or parclose, which blocked the doorway where the recording trumpet had been so recently. He could see through the squint that the Mass was continuing, but when he finally mastered the trick of opening the parclose he found himself suddenly back in the twentieth century and pitch darkness of his own vestry.

Bitterly disappointed, and now shivering a little with the cold night, he left the church by the west door, as he would normally do. . . only to find that he could again hear the sounds of the Mass outside.

To his amazement Miss Wilkins was waving and calling him from the vestry roof and clearly her recorder was playing-back the sounds of those ghostly monks recorded via the chantry flue whence the clouds of incense were intended to rise straight to heaven. Unmindful of his inadequate attire for a rendezvous with a lady, Mr Batchel climbed nimbly up the ladder and was about to clasp her helping hand, when his slipper came off and he fell backwards and down.

The fall seemed to take a long time, and instead of hitting the ground, he *woke* to the morning in his bedroom; on top of his bed but not between the sheets which were very crumpled. His slipper and stockings were still on his feet though, and a little damp. Mr Batchel dived off the bed, dressed hastily, finding his missing slipper (also damp) at the foot of the staircase, and rushed round to the vestry and Miss Wilkins's platform.

Severe disappointment awaited him, however. There was no wax cylinder on the machine, for even the warmth of springtime sun under a tarpaulin would soften the wax! And the prudent Elspeth had taken her spare cylinders home.

She was not very interested in Mr Batchel's dream, simply making some ribald remark about 'Getting to believe me that the de Villechins endowed Thorney Abbey, eh?' and advised him to 'Take more water with your night-cap.' When he protested, she continued. . .

'You dreamed it all. Your mind is full of the history of this place, and must have a good notion of what it was like. It simply supplied the setting to order, that's all . . .'

Mr Batchel was unwilling to relinquish the vividness that remained with him. In his experience dreams faded from daytime recollection. This adventure did not. He could picture the monks, the altar (which *had* been beneath the crude flue) and the wafer-box and chalice that had caught his eye.

Miss Wilkins was concerned only about the recording and was now testing the chimney aperture by calling to Jenkins, stationed below, and preparing to make a trial recording. Mr Batchel was with Jenkins in the vestry, and heard her muffled tones booming out from the fireplace . . . then an exclamation of annoyance.

'What's the matter?' he called up the chimney.

There was no reply, but a few moments later a tousled and annoyed Elspeth came in through the vestry door.

'I've dropped my bracelet down the chimney . . . has it come down here? The church has had enough of my family property!'

It had not, of course, and Miss Wilkins immediately 'volunteered' Jenkins (a small man) to go up the flue and find it. As can be imagined he was not too keen and Mr Batchel effaced himself until the matter was resolved and Jenkins started on his reluctant ascent.

They could hear his muttering—rather muffled—and indeed still see his boots while his progress, made in rather pot-holing style, was marked by a trickle of sooty dust and mortar of some sort, plus not a few birds' nest components. However, the bracelet suddenly tinkled down, followed in a rush by Jenkins clutching some other filthy bits and pieces.

He was taken outside to expectorate and to cough and brush up, for he looked like a chimney-sweep and had swallowed much dirt in the process.

'Twas on a ledge that crumbled away,' he said, 'just off the ground. I put my foot on it and it gave. These bits was there too. . .'

You will not, I think, need telling that although extremely damaged by years of smoke and heat, and devoid of all lustre, they were the waferbox and plate that Mr Batchel had seen in his dream. The vestry had, indeed, yielded up a little of its history to him.

There on the box, was the outline of the Boar's Head of the Villechins. Miss Wilkins took it in amazement.

'Family treasure—pre-Reformation, too, by heavens! I'll have this restored for the museum.'

Mr Batchel coughed. . . 'They belong to the Church,' he said quietly.

'Pah!' said Miss Wilkins. Then she winked, handing them back to the vicar. 'You churchmen are all alike. . . and you, Batchel, are no better than the Abbots of Thorney!'

(It seemed almost an anti-climax when an excellent recording was obtained of the choir's anthem. Perkins felt that both were too absorbed by the 'finding of a few old pots in that chimbley,' than by the miracle of sound recording.)